"I love your smile," Nicki said huskily, tracing the curve of Val's lips with the edge of her fingernail. "It makes you look wicked and sexy and *bad*."

"Bad?" he murmured. "That's good?"

"Very good. Good girls love bad boys."

He touched the tip of his tongue to the pulse at the base of her throat, very softly. "And are you a good girl?"

"I hope so." She gasped as his hands slid down her back, tracing the hollow of her spine, pulling her against his body. "I'm not exactly a fountain of experience."

His mouth dipped to hers for an exquisite swirling kiss. "Neither am I," he said. "Not this experience. Everything feels new to me. I can hardly"—his tongue followed the lush outline of her lips—"wait to see what happens next."

Nicki gazed into dark eyes burning with sensuality, love, amazement—and her. She loved seeing her reflection in his eyes. "Let's find out. . . ."

WHAT ARE *LOVESWEPT* ROMANCES?

They are stories of true romance and touching emotion. We believe those two very important ingredients are constants in our highly sensual and very believable stories in the *LOVESWEPT* line. Our goal is to give you, the reader, stories of consistently high quality that may sometimes make you laugh, sometimes make you cry, but are always fresh and creative and contain many delightful surprises within their pages.

Most romance fans read an enormous number of books. Those they truly love, they keep. Others may be traded with friends and soon forgotten. We hope that each *LOVESWEPT* romance will be a treasure—a "keeper." We will always try to publish

LOVE STORIES YOU'LL NEVER FORGET
BY AUTHORS YOU'LL ALWAYS REMEMBER

The Editors

Loveswept 587

Tonya Wood
Sneak

BANTAM BOOKS
NEW YORK · TORONTO · LONDON · SYDNEY · AUCKLAND

SNEAK
A Bantam Book / December 1992

If you would be interested in receiving protective vinyl
covers for your Loveswept books, please write to this address
for information:

Loveswept
Bantam Books
P.O. Box 985
Hicksville, NY 11802

ISBN 0-553-44316-X

Published simultaneously in the United States and Canada

Bantam Books are published by Bantam Books, a division of
Bantam Doubleday Dell Publishing Group, Inc. Its trademark,
consisting of the words "Bantam Books" and the portrayal of
a rooster, is Registered in U.S. Patent and Trademark Office
and in other countries. Marca Registrada. Bantam Books, 666
Fifth Avenue, New York, New York 10103.

PRINTED IN THE UNITED STATES OF AMERICA

OPM   0 9 8 7 6 5 4 3 2 1

Prologue

It was a beautiful night for breaking and entering.

It was snowing heavily, which was very nice for covering up telltale footprints. Visibility was limited to your hand in front of your face, and driving on the snow-packed roads was treacherous. The boys in blue would have their hands full taking care of fender benders and stranded motorists. They certainly wouldn't have time to worry about the notorious Jimmy Valentine, jewel thief at large.

Besides, it was Christmas Eve. There was a certain something in the air, a festive feeling of merriment and well-being. Nothing could possibly go wrong on a night like this.

Tools were packed carefully in a small leather pouch—gleaming silver picks of varying sizes, wire cutters, a tiny but powerful flashlight. Everything a self-respecting burglar would need for an enjoyable night on the town.

At half-past eleven the indispensable black leather coat was donned, along with soft kid gloves. Last but not least, a tasty cup of wassail was raised and a solitary toast made to ingenious entrepreneurs.

It was a beautiful night for breaking and entering.

One

Hell's bells. There was a burglar in her apartment.

Nicki Sharman's heart throbbed to a panicked beat as she stood in the shadows of the living room, paralyzed with shock. In the hallway she could see the faintest light spilling from her open bedroom door, hear the scratching, muffled sounds a very large mouse might make. Or a burglar busy at work.

She had suspected something was amiss when she had returned home from the Devonshires' Christmas Eve party and found her front door slightly ajar. Still, it wouldn't have been the first time she had forgotten to lock her door. She had a choice between playing it safe and calling for one of the nattily dressed private security guards who patrolled the building or crossing her fingers and investigating a bit further on her own. Nicki, being Nicki, crossed her fingers and tiptoed ahead.

As her eyes adjusted to the darkness, she could

see muddy footprints the color of Washington slush staining her exquisite Herez rug. Her wide mouth tightened, slanted eyes flashing blue fire. And then, incredibly, from the bedroom she heard a cheerful whistling—"Santa Claus Is Coming to Town". . . .

That did it.

Quietly she slipped out of her slim Italian heels and armed herself with a terra-cotta sculpture from the antique chest in the alcove. In the back of her mind a prudent voice suggested that this would be the appropriate time to retreat and summon a big strong man to assist her; Unfortunately she had had one too many glasses of eggnog to practice prudence. Besides, Nicki had been a fierce little tomboy long before her metamorphosis into a polished socialite. She was outraged that her beautiful sanctuary had been violated—on Christmas Eve, no less—and her strongest instinct was to fight back. One thwack over the head with a thirty-pound Qing Dynasty war-horse would teach the lawless vandal a little respect for the season of peace and goodwill.

He was still whistling, which annoyed her no end but helped disguise any noise she made sneaking down the hall. Just before she reached the bedroom, she paused, pressing herself flat against the peach-colored walls. The next step would commit her. Once she made her presence known, anything could happen.

The burglar stopped whistling and started singing the song in a husky whisper.

Nicki took a deep breath, then cautiously peered around the doorway. The broad-shouldered, dark-clad figure was down on one knee, his back to the door. It took Nicki a moment to realize that her burglar was taking time out from plundering and pillaging to tie his sneaker.

The pale cast of Nicki's complexion darkened to a burning flush. This was her chance. She hoisted the war-horse high above her head and lunged into the room. Her toe caught the corner of her bed, and her eyes watered with pain, but she never faltered in her attack. Still, the burglar must have caught sight of her through the corner of his eye; at the last second he gasped and tried to duck sideways. Nicki's heart was drumming like a piston in her chest, but she brought the sculpture down on the side of his head with all the force her 105-pound body could muster. The figurine gave its all for the effort, shattering into a million tiny shards. Stunned, the intruder teetered in his prayerlike position for a long, anxious moment, and Nicki wondered if she wouldn't have to sacrifice the Lladro sculpture on the dresser and hit him again. Fortunately it wasn't necessary. The burglar muttered something that sounded like "Bah, humbug" in a slurred voice, then tumbled face-first into a boneless sprawl on the deep pile carpet. Terra-cotta dust billowed in tiny mushroom clouds, then settled again like dark snow in his tangled hair.

Although he appeared quite unconscious, Nicki approached him cautiously. In a past lifetime, in those uncertain days before she'd become accustomed to Herez rugs and Italian heels, she had learned that appearances were usually—if not always—deceptive. She knelt, slipping her fingers beneath his hair and feeling the side of his neck for a pulse. It was strong and steady, as if he were taking a nice nap. She stood, a diminutive figure in a shimmering Gianni Versace gown, looking down at him with an expression of smug satisfaction on her face. "Let that be a lesson to you, nasty man. Uninvited houseguests make me irritable."

Naturally she intended to call the police, but she couldn't take the chance of him waking up in the meantime. She went to her closet, pulled a half-dozen belts off dresses and hooks, then set about securing her captive. "Pervert," she muttered, tying his feet together at the ankles with the silk sash from her bathrobe. "Degenerate. Looking through my private things." She crossed his hands behind his back and secured them tightly with a silver rope belt. "And on Christmas Eve, you devil. There, now. You aren't going anywhere till the police come and take you away."

He groaned and mumbled something unintelligible into the carpet. "I hope your head aches till New Year's," Nicki snapped, giving his large body a wide berth as she crossed to the telephone on the nightstand. She picked up the receiver and dialed 911, sitting on the edge of the bed with her legs crossed at the knees.

A disembodied female voice answered on the third ring. "Emergency Dispatch."

"I'd like to report a burglar in my apartment," Nicki said. She noticed that one of her nails had been chipped during the ruckus. She cradled the receiver between her shoulder and chin and picked up a nail file from the bedside table.

"Are you alone on the premises?"

"No." She frowned, carefully smoothing the jagged

edge of her nail. "I just told you. I have a burglar with me. I tied him up."

A pause. "Address?"

"I'm in the Sheffield Building on Fifth Street, just south of Devereaux Square—"

"Arraghh . . . uggh . . . my head . . ."

Santa Burglar was waking up. Nicki slanted him an amused glance through the web of her lashes, wanting to savor the moment he realized he was a prisoner of designer belts and scarves. He groaned and turned his head sideways, and all at once she had her first good look at his face. She met his gaze and smiled sweetly, wiggling her fingers at him. His eyes stretched almost comically; apparently her burglar was stunned to discover himself a captive of the so-called weaker sex. His features tightened with conflicting emotion, more than she could easily identify. The face belonged to a fallen angel: dark, dark brown eyes without a single fleck of gold, stark cheekbones, a mouth shaped in erotic, brooding lines. His hair was quite unusual, an uneven mixture of creamy brown and dark blond. It tumbled over his broad forehead in expert layers; obviously he made enough money in his chosen profession to afford a talented barber. He was not a homely burglar. He was a very attractive burglar.

And a very familiar one.

Realization struck her. The nail file dropped through Nicki's numbed fingers to the carpet. The telephone receiver slipped off her shoulder and bounced on the bed. Dear heaven. It couldn't be. But those eyes, those wicked Gypsy eyes . . . it had to be him. Val Santisi.

"Take a deep breath," the familiar burglar said. "You look like you've seen a ghost."

She took a deep breath, then another, staring at Val Santisi with owlish intensity. There he lay, trussed up like a turkey on her bedroom floor. The last time she had seen him, he had been a man-boy of eighteen, with jeans that drooped low on his skinny hips and mayhem in his unholy smile. He had filled out and grown up in the past thirteen years, though obviously he hadn't been tamed.

"Val?" she croaked hoarsely. *"Val?"*

"Hullo." He lay with his cheek on the carpet, bright-eyed and quite pleasant. "Long time no see."

She touched her fingers agitatedly to her chin, then her throat. "I don't believe you're here . . . like this. . . ."

"It's a shock for me too," he said.

Nicki suddenly became aware of the muffled shouts coming from the telephone receiver. She stared at it for a moment, chewing on her lip, then, before she could change her mind, hung it up. Once upon a time, Val Santisi had been a friend. She wasn't prepared to turn him in to the police, not yet. She needed time to think.

"It's not nice to make prank calls to 911," Val observed from his belly-flop position. "I think it's a federal offense."

A burglar with a conscience. "You should know," she said distractedly, shaking her head as if to clear it. "Tell me something, Val. Do you do this kind of thing regularly now, or just on holidays?"

"What a question." He sighed, his chiding tone indicating he had no intention of answering it. "You've still got that funny voice, Squeaky . . . Lauren Bacall with a touch of laryngitis. I thought you'd grow out of it."

Squeaky. She had almost forgotten that despised nickname. There had been a time when Val had been the only one allowed to call her Squeaky without putting himself in danger of a bloody nose. He had always treated her with the careless affection of an older brother, and she had always respected his bravado and ingenuity. Tonight Nicki thought it might be time to change the rules and finally pop him one.

She stood up, shaking back her cloudy black hair and squaring her bare shoulders. "I'd like to say it's nice to see you, but the circumstances leave a little to be desired."

"Brat," Val murmured, amusement glinting in his heavy-lidded eyes. "Listen to the way you say your vowels now, drawing them out like warm taffy. It's really something. The last time I saw you, you were fourteen years old and had a vocabulary of swear words a sailor would have envied. It's a miracle I even recognized you. Untie me, and we'll catch up on old times."

"Catch up on old times? Well, what an absolutely *lovely* idea." She paced an exasperated half-circle around him, her lower lip jutting out with a perturbed fullness. "And after we chat a bit, we'll have a slice of fruitcake and sing Christmas carols together. Won't that be jolly?" Then, in an entirely different voice: "Damn you, Val Santisi, I ought to toss you off the balcony! How *dare* you break into my home?"

"Don't get emotional. You know you lose your voice

when you get emotional." After several tries Val managed to turn over on his side. "Besides, you don't really want to toss me off the balcony. You've already knocked me out cold and tied me up. Be content, O terrifying Squeaky."

"Give me one good reason why I shouldn't call the police!" Her voice was going.

He eyed her thoughtfully. "All right, honey child. If you called the police, they would arrest you."

She made a sound between a laugh and a croak. "Arrest *me*? Why on earth would they arrest me?"

"For assaulting an officer and obstructing an investigation."

She stepped back a bit. "What? *What*? Would you repeat that, please?"

"I'm a police officer, Squeaky—Detective Val Santisi, Ninth Precinct, sworn to protect and serve the citizens of our nation's capital. Will you untie me now? This is a completely unnatural position. My feet are going to sleep. You're going to feel terribly guilty if my toes have to be amputated."

Nicki's expression went from shock to disbelief to helpless amusement. "A *police officer*? This is Nicki you're talking to, remember? I knew you back when you carried a fake I.D. and worked the blackjack tables in Atlantic City. Eighteen years old and the fastest hands in the business."

"I've always believed if a thing is worth doing, it's worth doing well."

Nicki gave a shaky laugh. "We grew up together. I don't remember you having any great desire to dedicate yourself to law and order. As a matter of fact, the last time I saw you, you were on your way out of town with Goodtime Grady's Traveling Carnival. You told me you were going to see the world and find out how gullible people could be. That doesn't sound like the police academy to me."

"And the last time I saw you, you were working in your daddy's fish market on Newton Street and had chipmunk cheeks full of chewing gum. You're not the only one who can change, Squeaky. Turn me loose, and I'll show you my badge."

"Ha! Fat chance."

Val let out an exasperated breath, flopping back on his stomach and scratching his nose against the carpet. "Look, enough is enough. I'm starting to itch. I think I'm allergic to this fuzzy rug of yours. My head is killing me, and I'm numb from the kneecaps down. Untie me."

"Let me see some identification first."

"How the hell am I supposed to show you my identification when you won't . . ." He paused, giving the carpet a muffled curse, hyphenated with a sneeze. Then he turned his head sideways and regarded her through narrowed eyes. "You were always damned stubborn. My identification is in my back pocket. If you wouldn't mind . . . ?"

After a second's hesitation Nicki stepped closer, eyeing the general area of his back pockets. Beneath the webbed waistband of his black leather jacket, firm buttocks gave beautiful shape to soft gray denim. It was quite obvious Val Santisi no longer needed a safety pin to keep his pants up.

She flicked an uncertain glance at Val, their gazes holding for a suspended moment. "Right pocket," he said.

The room settled into a thick silence. Nicki exhaled with resignation, then hitched up her narrow skirt and wiggled into a kneeling position beside him. It wasn't easy. Her dress was more style than substance, and Val wasn't the only one who had filled out during the past thirteen years. She stretched out her hand, her palm tingling above his right rear pocket.

"The anticipation is killing me," Val murmured.

Nicki scowled and pushed her fingers into the snug warmth of his pocket. There wasn't much room for exploring. She could almost feel the softness of his skin through the well-washed denim, the heat and gently rounded muscle beneath. She could also feel the instinctive tightening of those muscles as her hand slipped deeper in the pocket. Dry-mouthed, she persevered until her fingers closed around something that felt like a tiny flat wallet. She pulled it out with the lightning speed of a master pickpocket.

"Bingo," Val said. "Now that wasn't so bad, was it?"

She flipped open the vinyl case and examined his identification. There was a small silver badge on one side, a photo I.D. on the other, and everything seemed to be in order. By some incredible twist of fate, it appeared that Val Santisi had dedicated himself to upholding the law. It was absolutely astounding.

"I'm in shock," she said. She pushed the I.D. back in his pocket, since there seemed nowhere else to put it. Then she said suspiciously, "Are you a very good policeman? It was awfully easy for me to sneak up and whack you over—"

"I'm a bloody wonderful policeman," he snapped. "If you don't untie me in two seconds . . ."

It took fifteen. She freed him of the scarves and belts, then scrambled to her feet and watched as he slowly, slowly heaved himself into a sitting position. For a moment he remained perfectly still, eyes closed, palms braced flat on the carpet for balance. Nicki stared at the colorful bruises blooming like a spring garden on his temple, and her blue eyes darkened with guilt. She might have killed him.

Typically she squelched her uncertainty and took the defensive. "This wasn't my fault. I thought you were a burglar. I was just protecting myself."

Val opened his eyes, one corner of his mouth curving ironically. "And you're very good at it." He took a moment to look at her, really look at her, from head to toe and every curve in between. His mouth pursed in a silent whistle. "Egads. The dress. The hair. And look at that posture—little chin up, shoulders back, steel in your spine. Little Squeaky Boggs has turned herself into Cinderella."

Nicki flushed, thinking back to the endless nights she had practiced walking, sitting, and standing with encyclopedias stacked three deep on her head. She wasn't going to admit it, though. Not on her life. "My last name isn't Boggs," she said. "It's Sharman now."

He held her gaze a moment, then looked away, rubbing the faint red marks on his wrists. "Interesting. And where is Mr. Squeaky on this snowy Christmas Eve?"

"I'm not married. I had my name legally changed seven years ago. I'm a writer now, and I thought

Sharman sounded more professional. I have a weekly column in the Society section of the *Observer* . . . 'Sneak'."

He arched one brow. "Sneak?"

"It's a gossip column," she said impatiently. "I report on society events, personalities, power plays . . . that sort of thing. Now will you please tell me why—"

"One surprise after another," Val said admiringly. "College?"

"All four years. I waitressed my way through. And now that the formalities are over, would you mind explaining why you broke into my apartment?"

"Help me up first." He held out his hand. The soft white light from the lamp on the bedside table cast an angelic glow over his tawny hair. "Pretty please."

Nicki grasped him by the wrist with both hands. "Don't stand too quickly," she warned.

Val had never been one to take advice. He stood up too quickly. His dark eyes grew wide as he stared at Nicki, the color draining from his face. "Uh-oh. The stars are coming out."

Nicki lunged for him, her arms closing tight around his waist as he slumped over like a rag doll. She staggered for balance, leaning into him, the tender weight of her breasts flattened against his chest. "I told you to take it slow! Did you listen? Do you *ever* listen? Are you all right?"

"I will be," he said into her hair. His hands were on her hips, holding her firmly in the cradle of his thighs. "Just give me one minute to get my balance."

She gave him his minute, intensely conscious of the intimate lineup of their bodies, the stinging crush of her belly and breasts against solid muscle. Solid, rippling, warmly intoxicating hollows and ridges. Her face was pressed against the soft gray sweater exposed by his open jacket, and she could feel the rhythm of his heart against her cheek. Fast. Hard.

"You have your balance now," she said hoarsely.

He pulled back slightly, his gaze whimsical. His hands traveled up her back and gave her shoulders a gentle squeeze. "Do I?" he asked. "I wonder. You're all grown up and bloody gorgeous, Squeaky Boggs. A real heartbreaker."

Val Santisi thought Squeaky Boggs was bloody gorgeous. Holy merry Christmas.

She turned away from him, nervously plucking at the clingy silver lace bodice of her cocktail dress. For a moment she *was* Squeaky Boggs again, far more comfortable with a fight than a compliment. And for the life of her, she could think of nothing to say.

But only for a moment. She had made something of herself, she thought fiercely, deliberately and painstakingly *made* something of herself. She was Nicki Sharman now; she knew how to dress, how to converse with intelligent, educated people, how to flirt and flatter. She could hold her own among Washington's glitterati, secure in the knowledge there was absolutely no trace of the girl she had left behind.

She took a deep breath, forcing herself to turn and look straight into his eyes. "I want an answer to my question, Val. What are you doing in my apartment?"

He placed his hand over his heart. "Falling under the spell of the most breathtaking, spirited, bewitching, fearless—"

"Bugger off." As soon as she'd said the words, she

could have bitten her tongue off. Refined ladies did not say "bugger."

His dark eyes were full of mirth. "Now there's my old Squeaky talking. You can take the girl out of the fish market, but you can't take the fish market out of the girl."

"Don't call me Squeaky." She stood with her hands in fists, her legs braced as far apart as her pencil-thin skirt would allow. "Are you going to answer my question or not?"

He pushed his hands into the pockets of his jeans, the gesture drawing her eyes to the well-worn fabric stretched tightly over his hips. "Yes, ma'am. Right away, ma'am. I was attending a party in the building, and a friend mentioned seeing a suspicious-looking character loitering outside Nicki Sharman's apartment. Naturally I had no idea Nicki Sharman and Squeaky Boggs were one in the same when I decided to check things out. I found your door ajar, so I came in to investigate. It didn't look as if anything had been disturbed, but the sliding glass doors in here were wide open. I figured something must have spooked our intruder, and he took off down the fire escape. I was locking everything up when you surprised me with my early Christmas present."

"I see," was all she said.

He looked profoundly disappointed. "That's it? No gratitude? No apologies for denting my skull? No ice pack for my aching head, no tender ministrations for my bruised ego?"

Her reaction was something of a novelty to him, Nicki realized with a wave of amusement. She wasn't surprised. Even as a teenager, Val Santisi's melting good looks had radiated sexuality the way a fire gave off heat. Nicki had been four years younger and preoccupied with her own struggles, but she hadn't been blind. Women of all ages adored Val. They pampered him, indulged him, kept his young male ego thriving and healthy. Maturity had only added to his powerful physical appeal, and she could only assume he was accustomed to a more appreciative audience than she was providing.

"I'm glad I didn't kill you," she said sweetly.

"So am I." He scowled, tenderly probing the bruise on his temple. "You know, this isn't the reaction heroes expect when they slay nasty dragons for helpless maidens."

"There are no helpless maidens in this room. Besides, you didn't slay the nasty dragon, you chased him down the fire escape." He looked truly miffed at that, and she had to smile. Poor man. He'd delivered his damsel from the clutches of a terrible fate—in a roundabout way—and his damsel wasn't cooperating as she ought. "I *am* sorry about your head, Detective Santisi. Your courageous heroics definitely rate an ice bag."

"Oh, don't go to any trouble," he said. "I'll just go on outside and bury my head in a snowbank."

Nicki tried futilely to keep her smile from growing. "Heroes shouldn't whine. It's unbecoming. I'll go to the kitchen and make you an ice pack. In the meantime why don't you wait in the living room? Next to the fireplace you'll find a very comfortable recliner I keep especially for injured heroes . . . with wounded egos."

Val crossed his arms over his broad chest, staring at her intently. Then he broke out in an engaging grin. "Bloody gorgeous," he said. "If I'd known the little girl who lived above Boggs's Fish Market was going to turn into Cinderella, I might have hung around the old neighborhood."

Once again that feeling rolled through her, a deep, startled pleasure. Unnerved, she turned and walked to the doorway. Grace and dignity became a conscious effort—with every step she concentrated on those imaginary encyclopedias balanced precariously on her head. "This won't take me long," she said. "While I'm at it, I'll get you a couple of aspirins. I imagine you're going to have a devil of a headache."

She left the room without a backward glance. Val's smile faded, his face going quite still.

"I imagine I will," he said.

"They'll be wondering what happened to you," Nicki said.

"Who?" Val's eyes were closed as he rested in the injured-hero's recliner. His head was tilted sideways, and a blue rubber ice bag covered the nasty lump on his temple.

"Your friends . . . at the party you told me about. I'm surprised they haven't come looking for you already." Nicki adjusted the thermostat on the wall, then walked over to the fireplace and straightened the Hubert Robert landscape above the mantel. She was too restless to sit down. "Do you want me to call them for you?"

"I'm an embarrassed police officer, not a helpless

invalid. There's no need for you to call my friends and make this little fiasco public knowledge." He opened his eyes and slanted her a thoughtful gaze. "I'll tell them I ran into a door."

Her lips twitched. "Original."

"You know I've always been creative." Val sighed and removed the ice bag, placing it on a magazine on the coffee table. "I'd better get back before they send out a search party for me."

Nicki frowned, stepping closer in case he needed help. "You're sure you're all right? I really wish you would let me call your friends and explain—"

"I'm fine." Other than wincing a bit when he got to his feet, he seemed quite steady. "I can't think when I've had a more interesting Christmas Eve. Squeaky Boggs was the last person I expected to assault me tonight."

She bristled, the soft rise of skin over her cheekbones heating with indignation. "Don't call me Squeaky. And I didn't assault you, I was just—"

"Protecting yourself. I know, I know." His chest lifted with a sigh. "Be a good girl and keep your doors and windows locked, Ms. Sharman. The number of robberies in this area has more than tripled in the past six weeks."

"I know. The cat burglar . . . Jimmy Valentine."

He made a face. "That guy has been getting the credit for every break-in from here to Cleveland. Thanks to creative journalism—no offense—the public has this romantic vision of a charming Cary Grant clone stealing from the undeserving rich. No one seems to remember there *are* other criminals here in Washington with productive careers."

Nicki stared up at him, head tilted at a pensive angle. "Do you think he was the one who broke into my apartment tonight . . . Jimmy Valentine?"

"I doubt it. Our fellow tonight pretty well bungled the job. My guess is that he was an amateur out to collect a few extra Christmas presents for himself." A faint smile tucked the sulky curves of his mouth. He lifted his fist, teasingly grating her jaw with his knuckles. It was a gesture he had used often in the long-ago past, a brotherly salute to Squeaky Boggs's notorious right hook. "Take care, my feisty friend. Now that I know where to find you, I'll be in touch. You and I have a few years to catch up on."

Nicki followed him to the door, trying to force the tension from her body. It struck her that she was experiencing uncertainty for the first time in years. She had grown up in less than ideal circumstances, a wary product of a fiery-tempered Irish father and a string of intimidated stepmothers. Since leaving home, she had focused all her energy on putting as much distance between Squeaky Boggs and Nicki Sharman as possible. Luxury, security, and knowledge were things to be explored, irresistible challenges for a curious and audacious soul. She had set her sights on a promising future of her own making, never doubting that the best was yet to come. But suddenly Val Santisi was back in her life again, with his gold-dusted hair and the devil's own charm in his eternal eyes. Their friendship had been one of the few bright memories of her childhood, and she was genuinely happy to know he was doing so well. On the other hand, the restless, lonely misfit he remembered no longer existed. Sometimes it seemed as if that other life had been something that happened to someone else, and she was determined to keep it that way.

"You're sure you'll be all right?" she asked, when Val paused at the open door and the silence grew awkward.

"As sure as anyone can be these days," he said. His expression was curious as he stared down at her. "You can't relax with me, can you? I wonder why."

Nicki opened her mouth to deny it, but he stopped her with a quick, hard kiss on her lips. "Merry Christmas, Squeaky. I'll be seeing you soon."

He was gone then, striding down the hall toward the elevator, whistling a slightly off-key version of "I Saw Mommy Kissing Santa Claus."

Nicki closed the door with infinite care, locked it, and latched the security chain. Then she turned and surveyed the room, blue eyes softly blurred and wide with feeling.

She touched her lips. They felt tender and acutely sensitive, as if the brief pressure of his mouth had somehow bruised her. And deep within, she was conscious of a more serious wound, a jagged tear in the smooth fabric of her safe existence.

All in all, a burglar would have been easier to deal with.

Val Santisi trudged along through the wind-drifted snow on the sidewalk, bare head powdered with flakes, eyelashes frosted white. He walked in circles, because his car was parked in the alley across the street from the Sheffield Building, and he didn't want to get too far away. The bitter cold seeped like ice water through his clothes, but he thought better when he walked.

Belatedly he remembered the leather gloves in his inside coat pocket. He stopped beneath the snow-dusted light of a streetlamp, working open the zipper of his jacket with chilled, stiff fingers. He pulled out the gloves, then let out his breath in a frosty cloud as three small white cards tumbled to the ground. He picked them up one at a time: a business card for Vince Sanborne, inspector for the Department of Health; a card for Vern Sanderson of Vern's Lock and Key; and a card for Vaughn Sanford, owner and operator of Bug-Busters Pest Control.

He brushed the snow off the cards and slipped them into his hip pocket, right next to his police badge. He was getting careless in his old age. He knew better than to carry more than one identification at a time. What would have happened if Nicki had decided to search his jacket pockets while he'd been unconscious?

Nicki. All grown up and outrageously beautiful, a slender, self-made princess with a spine of tempered steel. Her solemn, rebellious mouth was fuller and softer than he remembered, her cheekbones more pronounced, her slight body rounded with a woman's curves. Had it not been for her eyes—those magnificent dark-lashed eyes that were almost too bright to look into—he would never have recognized her. He was still reeling.

He tugged on his gloves, his breath coming in dry, stinging gusts. His muscles began to rattle in convulsive, rhythmic shudders. He couldn't stay out in the cold much longer. Besides, he was getting nowhere, literally and figuratively.

He glanced up at the lighted windows of the Sheffield Building and made a sound deep in his throat, halfway between frustration and helplessness.

This was a hell of a time to develop a conscience.

Two

Nicki was hammering away on her video terminal when Dylan Lichter poked his shaggy blond head into her office.

"You there," he said, pointing an accusing finger. "It's Christmas Day. Only lowly reporters such as yours truly are expected to work today. Go home where you belong and make merry."

Nicki waved him away with one hand, kept typing with the other. "I can't. I'll miss my deadline."

"Your column isn't due until tomorrow."

"And I didn't even start it until this morning."

Dylan walked in and rolled up a chair next to her desk. He was wearing a brand-new shirt, new shoes, new cardigan, new watch, and a powerful new cologne. Obviously he and his family had already exchanged Christmas presents. "What do you mean, you didn't start until this morning? How long have you been here?"

Nicki glanced at the clock on the wall. It was nearly two in the afternoon. She had flagged down a lonely cab to take her to the office at half-past eight. "Not long. The snowstorm played havoc with my computer at home, so I had to work here. Don't worry about me, lowly reporter. I don't plan on staying here all day. By the way, Merry Christmas."

"Merry Christmas to you, too, glorified columnist. Have you had a nice holiday so far?"

"Wonderful. Now if you wouldn't mind letting me get back to work . . ."

"My mother gave me a hamster," Dylan said. "She said it made her sad to think of me living all alone in my apartment."

Nicki flicked him an amused glance. Baby-face Dylan was amazingly well adjusted for a reporter, eternally cheerful, and never at a loss for words. Unfortunately his flowery "Pollyanna" style of journalism usually landed him on the food pages. Dylan could make a meat-loaf recipe sound like manna from heaven. "Poor Dylan. Is Mommy still pressuring you to find a nice girl to marry?"

Dylan grinned, hazel eyes merry behind wire-rimmed glasses. "Nice, not so nice . . . Mommy isn't particular at this point."

"I have a feeling you haven't told her about Serena Grace," Nicki murmured. Dylan's weekly dates with Washington's infamous exotic dancer were a source of lively speculation around the newsroom. Senators and congressmen fought for the beauteous Serena Grace's attentions, yet sweet Dylan Lichter had been monopolizing the lady's Friday evenings for the past two months. When pressed for information, Dylan would only smile . . . and smile, and smile.

"Who the dickens is Serena?" Dylan asked, pinking around the ears.

"You little devil." Nicki turned back to her terminal. "I have work to do, Casanova. Return to the bosom of your family and roast some chestnuts or something, would you, please? I need peace and quiet here."

Dylan stood up, pushing his hands deep into the baggy pockets of his slacks. "Your wish is my command, grossly overpaid colleague. Like my new pants? My great-aunt Germaine gave them to me. She's a terrific lady. She's in a wheelchair, but she orders all her Christmas presents through the Sears catalog. The argyle socks were a gift from my cousin Gus. They have built-in odor-eaters. My great-aunt Patty knitted the sweater—she's practically blind, but she knits like a fiend—and my nephew Gordy gave me some great cologne. Polo . . . can you smell it?"

"Oh, yes."

"I made a haul, I'll tell you. We have a family party that lasts for three days. What about you?"

Nicki kept typing. "What about me?"

"Were you with your family, or . . . someone?"

Someone. An image entered her mind, eyes as dark and mysterious as woodsmoke, a teasing, elusive smile . . . her fingers stilled on the keyboard, and she stared at the monitor. Finally she said huskily, "I went to the Devonshires' Christmas Eve party."

"Ambassador Devonshire? You do run in lofty circles." He started fiddling with the pencil tucked above his ear, a sure sign that his inquiring mind was shifting into high gear. "That doesn't surprise me, though. Not only do you wield the pen that tweaks the high and mighty in your column, but you obviously have the credentials to carry it off."

Nicki smiled at that. "Credentials?"

Dylan's head bobbed. "You bet. When you've grown up squashed in the middle of the middle class, you can smell a pedigree a mile away. I knew the first time I met you that you were a class act."

A class act. Nicki wondered what her discerning friend would say if he knew she had spent her girlhood years living in a three-room apartment above a fish market. No wonder he could smell her pedigree.

She shoved herself to her feet, put her hands on Dylan's shoulders, and propelled him firmly toward the door. "Thank you for the compliment, Dylan. Don't be offended, but I'm sending you on your way now."

"I'm not offended," Dylan assured her over his shoulder. "It's been a pleasure spending this time with you, and I wish a very Merry Christmas to you and yours."

"The same to you."

Dylan did an unexpected about-face in the doorway and frowned down at her. "Look, I know this is none of my business, but . . . you've never mentioned your family. The idea of anyone being alone on Christmas—"

"I wasn't alone last night, Dylan." Oddly, she thought of Val Santisi rather than the crush of friends at the Devonshires' party. "I wont' be alone tonight, either, so put your mind at rest. I'm invited to dinner at Congressman Holt's. On New Year's Eve, I'll be at the Knights' party. My appointment book is full from now until spring. It's one of the perks of being a gossip columnist."

"I'm sorry. For a minute there I thought . . . well, who cares what I thought?" Dylan threw up his ropy arms. "I'm an idiot. Nicki Sharman, alone on Christmas? I apologize. I ran amok. Maybe I was just hoping I could take you home to dinner and give my family something to talk about besides everyone's favorite thief, Jimmy Valentine. Can you believe what he got away with last night? Talk about a haul."

"What?" Nicki's jaw dropped. "There was another robbery last night?"

"Was there ever. The Haskell mansion was burglarized while Thomas Haskell was . . . well, come to think of it, he was at the same party you attended— the Devonshires'. A silent alarm went off, but our sneaky friend managed to break into a safe and make off with over a hundred thousand dollars' worth of jewelry before the police arrived." Then, curiously: "The police tracked down Haskell at the Devonshires' party and told him what had happened. I'm surprised you didn't know."

"I left early," Nicki said slowly. "Dylan . . . what time did this happen?"

"The alarm went off at one A.M. I'm working up a piece on the robbery right now. Since we have a skeleton staff today, I got the story. It makes a refreshing change from the Women's section, I can tell you."

One o'clock. And the Haskell mansion was less than two blocks from the building where she lived, Nicki thought. The timing was right. If Jimmy Valentine had somehow obtained a list of guests attending the Devonshires' Christmas Eve party, he would have known exactly who would be away from home. When Val interrupted him at Nicki's apartment, he simply could have trotted on over to the next house on his list. It was possible.

Dylan was staring at her intently, his arms folded across his chest. "Nicki . . . do you know something I don't know? You're awfully quiet."

Nicki shook her head. After all, she had no concrete proof that it had been Jimmy Valentine who had broken into her apartment. And as Val had pointed out, he certainly wasn't the only burglar prowling the posh residential areas of Washington. In any case, the last thing she wanted to do was discuss the entire incident with motor-mouth Dylan. "I'm just surprised. I know the Haskells well. They're lovely people."

"Well, I hope those lovely people were insured," Dylan replied. "I'd better let you get back to work. Have a holly jolly, m'dear."

"'Bye, Dylan." Nicki closed the office door, then turned and walked slowly back to her desk. She sat down and tried to remember what she had been thinking, what she had been writing about, when Dylan had interrupted her, but she was too distracted to work. Such conflicting feelings crowded her mind: bittersweet memories stirred by an old friend's smile, a wobbly sense of anticipation, wistful thoughts of crowded houses and laughing families, curiosity about the man—the *men*—who had invaded her apartment last night, a vague foreboding she had no way of explaining.

She stood and walked to the window, wrapping her arms around her slight body as she stared at the city of white. The snow-packed roads were practically deserted. Her vivid imagination kicked in, offering the *Twilight Zone* fantasy that she had awakened this morning to find herself utterly alone on a silent, frozen planet. Isolated, desolate, doomed . . .

She sighed and shivered, derailing that particular train of thought. Instead of standing with her nose pressed against a cold plate of glass, she wished she were home in front of a glowing, fragrant fire. She would burrow into a soft, fuzzy afghan and eat hot buttered popcorn. Warm and cozy, safely hidden away from Old Man Winter. It was that sort of day.

Christmas melancholy, that's all it was, the time of year when hearts tried to reconcile what was with what could have been. Everyone suffered from it now and again. She would survive.

She always did.

In Nicki's opinion, the Knights' New Year's Eve party was a smashing success, with one glaring exception—the seafood buffet.

The Knights were serving crab, lobster, mahimahi, shrimp, and scallops in cream sauce. Nicki hated fish. She'd hated it while she was growing up, when she'd been forced to eat it at least once a day, and she hated it now. She would have given her diamond-stud earrings for a hot dog smothered with sauerkraut.

Sadly the lowly hot dog was seldom served at elegant Washington social functions.

She'd done her work for the evening, mingling with politicians and captains of finance, media moguls and hangers-on, gathering the latest tittle-tattle while her sources were still sober enough to be reliable. At the moment she was standing in the shadows of the huge staircase that curved upward three stories, observing the expensive dazzle of the Knights' guests as they moved about like bright, exotic birds. It was still hard to believe she was a part of it all. She sometimes found herself holding her breath, waiting for someone to recognize Squeaky Boggs from Newton Street beneath her Elizabeth Arden makeup and the gossamer midnight-blue slip-dress from Giorgio Armani.

She caught sight of herself in the gilt-edged mirror across the entry hall. She smiled, not because she was pleased with what she saw, but because she looked as if she belonged in this elegant home, with its Oriental rugs and glowing, dark-paneled walls. Her hair was down, framing her face in a shimmering wave, her eyes softly emphasized with azure shadow, a simple rhinestone choker at her throat. As she had made her life over, made herself over, she had discovered a very important lesson—less is more. Simplicity was her personal trademark. It was difficult to find fault with pure, beautiful color and fluid, body-skimming lines. And it was important that no one find fault.

"Nicki?" A gentle hand touched her arm, a softly accented voice spoke over her shoulder. "You are hiding from the nasty fish smells once again? I do not understand your aversion for the lobster. Everyone enjoys the lobster."

Nicki turned to smile at her date for the evening, Philip Rafi, a well-known Washington heart specialist. Although he was older than she by more than fifteen years, he possessed a delightful sense of humor and an old-fashioned courtliness she found endearing. He had the strikingly handsome features of his Arabic ancestors; this, combined with an impressive personal fortune, made him a favorite of Washington hostesses. Nicki was always amused by the lighthearted banter the two of them did so well. And if ever Philip desired a more intimate relationship, he was wise enough to bide his time. Unlike other men Nicki had known, Philip lived life at the most leisurely pace, thoroughly enjoying whatever the moment offered.

"I also enjoy the lobster," Nicki said, "as long as it is swimming happily in an ocean far away from me."

Philip sighed, pushing his hands in the pockets of his double-breasted taupe evening jacket. This was the third party he had escorted Nicki to during the holiday season; unfortunately, fish had been served on every occasion. "You must eat every now and then—it is a simple fact of life. I am a doctor, I know these things. On the way home we will stop at a little Italian restaurant I know. I will not have my date facing the New Year on an empty stomach."

A combination of amusement and gratitude sparkled in her eyes. "You're a wonderful friend and a true gentleman," she said, rising on tiptoe to brush a light kiss on his cheek. As she did, she caught sight of the man standing directly behind them. Her lips froze in a polite pucker on Philip's jaw.

Val Santisi?

She pinched her eyes shut and then looked again, but he was still there. He was wearing a beautifully cut black tuxedo and a white dress shirt that contrasted sharply with his golden complexion. His luminous eyes held a look as innocent and guileless as a newborn babe's. His name was on her lips, but she could make no sound.

"Not such a gentleman." Philip laughed, stepping back to include Val in the conversation. "I forget my manners. I brought someone to meet you, Nicki. I knew you would find him most interesting, considering the robberies we have heard so much about lately. He is a private security analyst from New York. The Knights are consulting him about designing a security system for their home. Nicki Sharman, may I introduce Virgil Sawyer. Mr. Sawyer, this is a very good friend of mine. . . ."

Nicki was no longer listening. Her eyes were diamond-bright as she stared at Val, soft lips parted in an expression of utter bafflement. Virgil Sawyer? A private security specialist?

Virgil/Val picked up her limp, lifeless hand. "How do you do, Ms. Sharman?" he said politely. "It's very nice to meet you."

I must have hit him harder than I realized, Nicki thought wildly. *I did permanent damage.*

"Nicki writes for the *Observer*," Philip was saying affectionately. "Every Wednesday she has us all on pins and needles, wondering where she will focus her oh-so-perceptive eye. Perhaps you've read her column?"

"I haven't had the pleasure," Val replied. "I only arrived in the city two days ago, and I'm afraid I haven't had time even to pick up a newspaper."

Nicki fixed him with a fierce stare. What did he mean, he'd only arrived in the city two days ago? She had cracked him over the head with a Chinese war-horse on Christmas Eve. He still had the bruises to prove it. Val lived in Washington, he worked there. . . .

Philip was looking at her strangely. Nicki realized her silence had gone on far too long, that it was imperative she collect her scattered wits. There was no help from Val. He smiled politely, waiting for her to show some sign of life. She became conscious of his fingers still gripping her hand, much too tightly for comfort.

He didn't want her to give him away.

She jerked her hand free, clapping it over her mouth to stifle a manufactured cough. "Excuse me," she choked out hoarsely. "I must have something caught in my throat. Philip, would you mind getting me a glass of water?"

"It would be my pleasure," Philip said promptly, ever the gentleman. "I won't be a minute. Please excuse me, Mr. Sawyer."

Val rocked up and down on his heels as he watched Philip make his way through the crowd. "A charming friend you have there," he remarked softly, with amusement. "A little old for you, though, wouldn't you say? Or is this more of a grandfather-grand-daughter relationship the two of you have going?"

His composure was aggravating. "You've got thirty seconds," Nicki hissed through a plastic smile as she nodded at a passing acquaintance. "Why are you calling yourself Virgil? Why are you masquerading as a security analyst? What are you doing here?"

He seemed not to have heard a word she said. He stepped closer, nudging her farther back behind the stairway. There was a mischievous curve to his erotic mouth. "Guess what?"

Nicki's hand lifted to the choker at her throat. It was, appropriately enough, choking her. With his luminous Gypsy eyes and remarkable gold-dusted hair, Val Santisi burned like a flame in a darkroom. His energy was a palpable thing; it shivered between them like the prickling quills of a sparkler. His amusement confounded her. His audacity infuriated her. In many ways Val Santisi hadn't changed at all from the cocky, incorrigible teenager she had once known.

She gave him her most ferocious scowl. "What do you mean, guess what? Guess what *what*?"

"It's nearly midnight, Squeaky my old friend. Listen."

She listened, never taking her eyes from his. For the first time she heard the laughing, excited voices raised in unison: "Five . . . four . . . three . . . two . . ."

"One," Val whispered.

The house exploded with cheers. Confetti flew. Noisemakers shrilled. Couples embraced. From outside in the streets came the sounds of horns honking and pans banging.

But the little alcove beneath the stairs was shrouded

in silence. Val stared at Nicki, his faint smile piercing her with its tenderness. His hand touched the soft sheen of her hair.

"Happy New Year," he said.

Slowly he bent his head and rested his forehead against hers. Nicki's gaze slid helplessly to his mouth, and a shaft of heat stabbed down through her body. For a moment she forgot the mysteries and lies; she could only wonder what it would be like to open up to his seeking mouth, to respond without inhibitions. What could a man like Val Santisi show her? What could he make her feel if she let down her guard . . . ?

He knew. She looked into his eyes, so close to hers, and knew he was well aware of the effect he had on her. Oh, he was good. But then, this dark-eyed menace had always had a way with women. He'd never bothered with little Squeaky Boggs before, but there was a first time for everything.

"Oh, no, you don't," she said hoarsely, more to herself than him. But when she would have turned away, his hand grasped the back of her neck, his mouth finding hers with a caressing intensity that could have melted cold lead. The kiss was everything and more than she had imagined it might be. His mouth played compellingly over hers, hungry and demanding, soft and unhurried. Their lips clung, mating, breaking contact, mating again. His tongue touched hers for the first time, inviting her to dance, and she made a husky, inarticulate sound deep in her throat. Her hands opened and closed convulsively on his shirtfront as her mouth drank from his. Their hips came together, and the contact was so exquisite that a shudder passed through her like a current. The sheer, almost painful pleasure gave her the strength to break away from the kiss with a soft, sucking sound. "Val, this isn't—"

"Shhh." He held her face in his hands and pressed a simple gentle kiss on the tip of her nose. "It was just a kiss. Just a Happy New Year's kiss from one old friend to another."

But when he lifted his head, she saw that his hair was tousled and his skin was flushed, and he'd lost that light of distant amusement that usually lurked in his eyes.

"Just a kiss," Nicki whispered. Tempting beyond belief, a fountain of earthly pleasure . . . but just a kiss.

They stood facing each other, still and watchful. Val looked as if he would have said something more, but suddenly Philip was back, pressing a glass of water into Nicki's hand and muttering apologies for the delay. "The clock struck twelve, and many women insisted on kissing me as I came from the kitchen," he explained with a heartfelt sigh. "It was a great trial to me. I hope Mr. Sawyer kept you entertained."

Nicki gulped at the water, and it sloshed over the side of the glass. "You're forgiven," she muttered, coloring as she brushed the drops from her chin.

"You may not forgive me when you hear my news," Philip replied. "I've been called to the hospital. An emergency. I'm afraid I have to leave right away."

"Pity," Val murmured.

"I don't mind waiting here for you, Philip." Nicki inwardly winced at the smoky, scratchy tones of her telltale voice. It was like raising a flag whenever her body chemistry started bubbling.

Philip pressed a hand over his heart in a gesture that seemed a bit corny to Nicki. "Regretfully, I'm afraid this could take hours. Emergency surgery. I apologize, my dear. I'll take you home on the way to the hospital."

"No!" The exclamation was so loud that both men stared at her in surprise. Coloring, Nicki added faintly, "The night is still young. I'll take a taxi home later."

"At least let me claim my New Year's kiss," Philip said. He leaned forward and pressed his lips to hers, gently at first, then with an increasing passion that made Nicki's eyes fly open. Over Philip's shoulder, she locked gazes with Val.

He didn't blink, didn't move a single muscle. He just stared.

Flustered, she pulled away from Philip and gave him a brilliant, shaky smile. "Call me tomorrow?"

"Of course." He raised her hand to his lips and gallantly kissed the tips of her fingers. "Good night, then. And, Mr. Sawyer, I'm sorry we didn't get a chance to talk. I would like to discuss a security system for my own home, when you have the time."

"I'll get in touch with you," Val promised, shaking the older man's hand.

Philip left. Nicki slowly turned her head and found Val's bright, speculative gaze on her. For a moment they stared at each other; then, as if of one accord, they turned and surveyed the laughing, chattering party-goers crossing from the living room to the dining room and back again. No one seemed to notice the quiet couple in the shadow of the stairs.

Val cleared his throat and ran a finger along the inside of his shirt collar. "I suppose you're going to want an explanation."

"Oh, you suppose right."

"This really isn't the best place to talk, Squeaky. Maybe tomorrow—"

"Not tomorrow. Tonight. And don't call me Squeaky."

A slow smile curved his mouth, though he continued to stare straight ahead. "Such a tough little Cinderella. All right, then. Tonight. We'll leave."

"Whatever it takes to get a few straight answers," Nicki said.

For a moment neither of them moved. Then Val pushed away from the wall, his hand touching the small of her back for a brief second. "I'll meet you out in front in five minutes."

Nicki watched him walk away, her fingers closing tightly over her bare arms. She studied the way his tough, wide shoulders filled out the elegant evening jacket, the way the light from the chandelier picked out the golden streaks in his unusual hair. Familiar, yet a stranger, with the secrets and experiences of thirteen years between them.

She took a deep breath and followed him.

Three

"You didn't bring a car?"

Nicki's voice was muffled by the turned-up velvet collar of her beaded cape. The tip of her nose was stinging cold, probably the first stages of frostbite. Drifting ice crystals filled the air, lighting the moonless night with a haze of glittering white.

"Did I say I brought my car?" Val shook the snowflakes off his hair and grinned down at her. From nose to ankles she was bundled in her swirling, sparkling cape, and a black scarf covered her head. He could see huge blue eyes and snow-dusted bangs, and not much else. The eyes, however, were very expressive—the word "venomous" came to mind. Squeaky was ticked off. "No. I'm sorry—I walked to the party tonight. Of course, it wasn't snowing then."

Nicki grabbed the sleeve of his wool overcoat as her delicate sling-back pumps did a wild tap dance on a patch of ice. "You told me you were taking me somewhere to talk!"

"And so I am, honey child." He put his arm around the portion of her voluminous cape that was most likely her waist, steadying her as she skidded along beside him on the icy sidewalk. "I enjoy taking walks on snowy evenings. It helps me think clearly. Don't you like to walk?"

"Some of us can . . . think c-clearly at room t-temperature." Something was happening to her lipstick. The bitter cold was turning it into Superglue, sticking her lips together between every syllable. "Besides, this is n-n-no night for a walk. You're just trying to distract me by freezing me to death. It w-w-won't work. I want answers. I want honesty. And I . . . want . . . a *taxi!*"

"Why didn't you say so? Your wish is my command, my little Eskimo pie." Val flagged down a passing cab, the first he'd seen since they'd left the Knights' town house. He was vastly relieved, though he didn't admit it. He'd forgotten what a challenge it could be finding a taxi on New Year's Eve.

"To Chuck and Fred's," Val instructed the driver, after he'd bundled Nicki into the cab.

The driver scratched his head, squinting in the rearview mirror. "I don't know any Chuck and Fred, pal."

Nicki stared at Val. "I don't know any Chuck and Fred either."

"So?" Val tipped back his head, looking quizzically down at her. Melting snowflakes dripped off the end of her little red nose. Her eyes were very wide and very blue and very, very suspicious. "Chuck and

Fred's happens to be a terrific place to eat. Don't look so skeptical, Squeaky. Did you think you were personally acquainted with every intimate little restaurant in this city?"

Nicki and the cabdriver replied in perfect unison, "Yes."

"Well, obviously *not*," Val replied, an unabashed grin lighting his dark face. "Let this be a humbling experience for you both. The corner of Mission and Vine Street, driver."

"Vine Street?" The cabdriver sounded dubious. "You're sure about the address? I don't remember seeing any fancy restaurants—"

"Meter's running." Val settled back against the seat and drew Nicki's shivering body into the curve of his arm. "Step on it, my friend. The lady and I have a lot of lost time to make up for."

"This isn't a date," Nicki said abruptly. Something about the way Val cuddled against her told her he needed to be reminded. "We're not out for a good time tonight, *Virgil*."

"We may have a problem there." Val bent his head, his lips next to her ear, and whispered softly, "I've never been very good at having a bad time."

Truer words were never spoken. Instead of sliding to the opposite side of the car, which she knew she should do, Nicki turned her head, her cold cheeks stinging with a sudden flood of heat. Her eyes were level with his mouth, with that come-hither smile that brought back the past with bittersweet vividness. Never had she met anyone who possessed such an irresistible hunger for life. As a child, she'd been mesmerized by his reckless passion for the cool ingenuity and fiery challenge of it. She still was.

She felt a whisper of long-buried pain that intensified the stress of being so close to him. Val had always thrived on the whims of fate, while Nicki had fought them tooth and nail. He'd once told her that happy people didn't believe in miracles. Regardless of the challenge or the risk, the sheer joy of the moment was the only miracle he ever needed. Nicki never understood how he did it. Happiness had always been elusive for her, a shadowy reward she had to work and wait for. Even now, despite the undeniable satisfaction of her achievements, she sometimes found herself still . . . waiting.

Nicki doubted Val Santisi had ever waited for anything in his life—least of all happiness. It wasn't in his nature.

Slowly she raised her gaze to his, expecting to find the familiar light of wicked amusement. Instead she intercepted a startling look of naked longing that flickered through her like wildfire. He didn't bother to hide it; his half-smile was heated and sleepy and vaguely diabolic.

"Happy, happy, *happy* New Year," he said softly. He brushed a kiss on the tip of her reddened nose, then drew back slightly, his smile growing infinitely more dangerous. "Welcome back to my life, blue eyes."

There was an inch of space, a moment of powerful suspension while he held her gaze. Each smothered breath Nicki took was a conscious effort. No one could turn on the heat like Val Santisi. He was a devastating combination of humor, experience, and stark sensuality. Was he trying to change his tactics now, distracting her by seducing her?

Probably.

He had another think coming. It was a little tiny fist, and Nicki planted it none-too-gently in his side. "I think you've confused me with Raye Ann Rudy," she said through her teeth.

He clutched his middle and stared at her, bright-eyed with shock and confusion. She wasn't respond-ing the way she should at all. "Raye Ann? Raye Ann who? What the devil are you talking about, you crazy person?"

"How quickly they forget." Nicki clucked her tongue and shook her head. "Raye Ann worked at the Big and Tall Shop across the street from the fish market. Six-two in her stocking feet, with all the hills and valleys of a substantial mountain range. Oh, *you* remember—the pretty blonde who was a pushover for a box of chocolate-covered cherries and a smooth line? I heard about the time the two of you snuck off to that nightclub in Atlantic City for amateur night, and Raye Ann ended up dancing on the—"

"*That* Raye Ann." Val made a strangled sound in his throat. "Who on earth told you those stories? You were just a kid, you couldn't have been more than thirteen years old when . . . never mind. Never mind. We're not going to talk about this. You're a devious and frustrating woman."

"Thank you." Nicki busied herself fluffing the folds of her cape. It was much safer dealing with a defen-sive Val than a charming, seductive, predatory Val. All she had to do was continue irritating him on a regular basis. She slanted him a creamy smile, fluttering her lashes. "Welcome back to my life, *brown eyes*."

He gave her an arrested look, as if seeing her for the first time, then suddenly lifted his hand and jerked her scarf down over her eyes. Only her luscious mouth was visible beneath the silky material, sassy and tempting with a beguiling grin.

"And heaven help us both," he said grimly.

"Hell no, they don't have *sushi*!"

Val glared at Nicki across a Formica table not much larger than a chessboard. His overcoat was slung over the back of his chair, the top two buttons of his shirt were undone, and his tie had been stuffed in his pants pocket. With his snow-wet hair tangled over his forehead, he looked very young and achingly familiar. "Does this *look* like a place that serves sushi?"

"Will you relax? I was only teasing." Nicki slipped her cape off her shoulders, arranging it over the vinyl-padded back of her chair. There were no coatracks at this intimate little restaurant. There were no candles on the tables, and the only music came from a radio on the counter next to the cash register. The specials of the day were listed on a huge chalkboard tacked to the wall beneath a flickering neon beer sign. In honor of New Year's Eve, Chuck and Fred were offering "Festive Fajitas with Party-Hearty Guacamole." Also in keeping with the spirit of the evening, three flagging helium balloons were anchored to the salt and pepper holders at each table. Nicki ducked her head sideways, trying to find Val through the low-flying bouquet. "You never used to take me so seriously."

"You've done some serious growing up." Val settled back in his chair, fiddling with the silverware on the table. Walking into Chuck and Fred's, it had occurred to him that Nicki Sharman might not appreciate his mischievous choice of a restaurant quite as much as Squeaky Boggs might have. He didn't know what to expect from her anymore. There was a savvy intelligence glittering in her beautiful blue eyes, an unmistakable strength of will barely disguised by her disarming smile.

If a man had something to hide, it could make him a little uneasy.

He cleared his throat, swatting at a balloon bobbing in front of his nose. "It's been more than ten years. You're not the same Squeaky Boggs who took pity on every stray cat in the neighborhood and fought like a hellion if anyone tried to make her wear 'girl clothes.'"

"People change . . . thank goodness. You have to grow, to challenge yourself, if you want to make your mark in this life."

In all his rowdy, devil-may-care, adventuresome thirty-two years, Val had never once indulged in worrying whether or not he was making his "mark" in life. Just *living* it had been enough, reveling in it, clinging to it as if it were a wild roller-coaster ride.

Till now.

"What about me?" he asked slowly, surprised that he felt the need even to ask the question. "Have I changed?"

"Oh, you've changed." She pushed the balloons to

one side, giving him a look that said she hadn't forgotten the reason they were there, despite his various efforts to distract her. "As a matter of fact, you keep changing right in front of my eyes. Your name. Your occupation. I can hardly wait to see who you are tomorrow."

So much for introspection, Val thought, shaking off his self-pitying mood. He was breathing, his healthy heart was beating steady and strong; it stood to reason his life was in fairly good shape. At the moment he would be wise to concentrate on the problem at hand.

"So?" Nicki prompted, subtly arching one dark brow.

"One minute," Val said. He untied the balloon bouquet with a flick of his wrist, his dark eyes following its slow, slow ascent to the ceiling. "I like to be able to concentrate without distractions when I'm trying to talk to someone. Chuck and Fred were slightly misguided here, tying helium balloons in the middle of the table. If somebody happened to light up a cigarette a little too close to—"

"I've been really cooperative, don't you think?" Nicki interrupted, drumming her fingers on the table. "I didn't give you away to Philip, I left the Knight's party early, I plodded through a blizzard like a faithful sled dog. . . ."

"You've been a trouper. You deserve a reward for being such a good sport. I'll order you Chuck and Fred's famous Philly steak sandwich with extra—"

"But I'm tired of your diversion tactics. I'm going to count to three, then I want you to start talking."

Val winced. "Don't count, Squeaky. I really hate it

when women count. I remember this teacher I had in middle school—"

"Don't call me Squeaky, and stop dodging the issue. Two . . ."

"All right. You want the truth, you'll have it." Funny the way his throat tightened like a vise on the words, but he forced his voice to push through. "But remember, I'm going against policy telling you all this. The Knights asked the police department for extra security for their guests tonight. All the press that Jimmy Valentine has been getting lately made them nervous. I agreed to work undercover—discreetly, of course—doing the mingle-and-munch bit while I kept an eye on things. At midnight, Sergeant McRoth—did you notice the stocky, red-haired guy who looked like he should have been wearing a kilt instead of a tuxedo? No? Anyway, he took over at midnight."

"It doesn't make sense," Nicki said slowly. "Why would the Knights worry about police protection? Their home isn't likely to be burglarized while they're entertaining guests."

"You wouldn't think so, but Jimmy Valentine is beginning to show some real creativity. Night before last, he visited a well-known Washington divorce attorney while a dinner party was in full swing. Twenty-two guests, yet no one saw anything unusual. Both safes in the house were cleaned out, a rare stamp collection was stolen from the library, and two thousand dollars in cash was taken from a cigar box hidden in the closet of the master bedroom. Our thief not only knew what he wanted but knew exactly where to find it."

Nicki was bewildered. "How could that be? The house is full of people, yet a perfect stranger somehow waltzes through all these rooms. . . ." Her voice trailed off, and a new light came into her eyes. She leaned forward, dropping her voice until it was a barely audible whisper. "Val? Are you thinking what I'm thinking?"

"I doubt it." Val swallowed hard, his dazzled eyes dropping helplessly to the shape of her breasts beneath the delicate half-shells of blue silk. Goose bumps shivered over his skin. He was no stranger to a woman's body, but Squeaky Boggs did something amazing for "girl clothes." Her skin was luminous, glowing like ivory over the upper swell of her breasts, warming to a dusky pink in the shadows between. He wondered if the cool silk felt as tantalizing as it looked, teasing and caressing her bare flesh. He wondered if the sensation aroused her.

He lifted his eyes and looked into hers, long and hard. One corner of his wide mouth quirked upward, bringing a dimple into play.

And he's looking straight at me, Nicki thought with a stab of panic. For a long, uncertain moment she returned that look, experiencing the powerful sensation of being drawn toward him, absorbed by him. Val's charm came easily and ran deep—witness the way her toes were curling inside her shoes. He was very clever with women—too clever—supremely self-confident and recklessly appealing. An adorable boy child, mysterious and heartbreaking, with his graceful, well-muscled body and sweetly erotic smile.

So tempting. She wasn't sure what scared her the most—succumbing or resisting. Until she knew, all she could do was cling to her conscious control and suppress the dark, crazy stirrings inside her.

"I realize I'm no policeman"—a definite squeak in her voice here, but nothing too humiliating—"but I've got a theory. What if there was a reason no one noticed anything out of the ordinary? What if one of the *guests* was Jimmy Valentine?"

Val stared at her. "What?"

"Think about it." She tried to ignore the dark, liquid eyes that seemed to be drinking her up. It wasn't easy. "A pillar of society, someone whose comings and goings would never be suspect. Someone who is intimately familiar with the homes and habits of his dear, wealthy friends. It makes sense. Maybe you should check into that."

"What a novel idea," Val said flatly, one hand coming up to massage the back of his neck. "Why didn't we police types think of that?"

"I suppose by that you mean you already have. Do you have a headache?"

Immediately he dropped his hand. "I don't get headaches. Ever. What's taking that waitress so long? We haven't seen a menu yet, and we've been waiting thirty minutes."

Nicki consulted her narrow silver watch. "Actually it's been . . . closer to six minutes."

"Thank you," Val said succinctly.

And so, for the moment at least, it was a draw. The waitress came and handed out plastic-laminated menus. Nicki held hers with both hands like a shield, intensely conscious of Val's physical presence: the way his long legs stretched out beneath the able, the faint smell of his cologne, a soft rustling as he shifted restlessly in his chair.

She didn't realize she was holding the menu upside down until the waitress helpfully pointed it out.

"I can't see a thing. Why don't you turn on the light?"

"I'm trying."

"What's that thumping noise?"

"That thumping noise is the sound of my hand trying to find the light switch on the wall."

"It's your apartment. You can't find the light in your own apartment?"

"I haven't lived here very long."

"I think you planned this deliberately."

"Clever girl. The blizzard was just a ploy to lure you to my luxurious bachelor pad. I knew half the roads in Washington would be closed tonight. I knew there wouldn't be a cab within five miles. I knew we'd have no choice but to hitch a ride to my apartment on a bleeding *snow plow.* Yes, sir, everything is going beautifully so far." Val finally located the light switch several inches above where it had been the night before. It was a three-in-one switch, controlling a floor lamp beside the sofa, a ceramic ceiling fixture, and the interior light in the corner curio cabinet. The small room blazed to life.

"Oh, my," Nicki said. "My, oh, my."

It was immediately obvious that Val had not planned on entertaining company. The place was a disaster. Clean laundry overflowed the sofa, apparently waiting to be folded. A week's worth of newspapers littered the coffee table, along with a couple of empty coffee cups and several candy wrappers. Socks of various colors were scattered wildly around the room, as if a certain someone had lost patience trying to find a match. A brown argyle swam with the goldfish in a small aquarium on the bookshelves.

"I spiffed up the place in preparation for the big seduction scene." Val shrugged out of his overcoat and tossed it on a wobbly brass coatrack. "Can I take your coat before I jump your bones?"

Nicki hesitated, then slipped her cape off her shoulders and handed it to him. "You're angry."

"I'm not angry." He could have told her there was a big difference between anger and frustration. All through the evening, he'd been almost painfully sensitive to every nuance of expression that crossed her face. Nothing escaped him, not the rhythm of her breath, not the way she caught her lip between her teeth when she was deep in thought, not the way she slipped her shoes off beneath the table when she thought no one was looking. He was receptive to the smallest, most insignificant detail, while Nicki seemed all but oblivious to him. He began to wonder if he'd imagined her response when he'd kissed her at the party. Wishful thinking?

Hell, no. He'd been taut and aching all the way to his toes, and he could swear she'd felt the same. Even now, deep muscles clenched painfully inside him.

"You're doing that thing again," Nicki said, watching him.

Val barely stopped himself from glancing at his nether regions. "What thing?"

"Rubbing your neck as if you have a headache."

He drew a deep breath and marched over to the sofa, scooping up an armful of laundry. "Squeaky, if and when I get a headache—which I won't, because real men don't get headaches—I promise you'll be the first to know. Make yourself at home. I'll fix some hot coffee to warm us up."

"How long do you think the roads will be impassible? Maybe if I called a cab now, they might be able to—"

"You're here till morning. We're lucky my place was so close, or we'd be spending the night at Chuck and Fred's. Now if you'll excuse me—"

"You dropped something," she said, nodding at a pair of baby-blue Jockey shorts on the floor.

Flushing, Val picked up the shorts and dropped a towel. He bent to pick up the towel and dropped practically everything else in his arms. He said a word that Nicki hadn't heard since she'd lived on Newton Street and sat down hard on the sofa.

"I'm not having a very good night," he said. Then, with a touch of wistfulness: "I could sure use a little TLC about now."

After a moment Nicki sat down beside him. She smiled faintly, rubbing her bare arms with stiff fingers. From his side Val stared at her with a silent watchfulness. Her hair was looped behind her ears, the way she'd worn it when she was thirteen. The fragile wing of her cheekbone was ruddy from the cold, and the scent of violets surrounded him in a sweet cloud of pleasure. His heart was pounding.

Then Nicki said, "I could sure use a friend about now."

He lifted his eyes to hers. "What did you say?"

"There aren't many people in Washington I feel safe with. This city has more than its fair share of schemers and manipulators and egotists. You have to be on your guard constantly. It's exhilarating, but it can be exhausting too." She let out a soft breath, struggling to keep her smile. This was so hard, when she wanted to gravitate to the heat of his body next to hers, when the deliberately sexual, questioning look in his dark eyes made her blush and tremble like a child. She was mesmerized by the power of his physical appeal; female curiosity was overwhelming her . . . and scaring her half to death. Friendship was her most obvious defense, an antidote to the erotic fantasies that burned her imagination.

"It would be nice to know a dependable friend is close by," she finished huskily.

For a moment he remained motionless. He thought he might be paralyzed. There were many things women had asked from him over the years, but he couldn't remember a single request for dependability. Neither could he remember a time when he had wanted a woman more than he did at that moment. She made him feel precarious and tormented and incredibly, wonderfully *alive.* There was an anticipation in him he had never known before; the wanting was like an open wound deep inside, scarring him with all its hunger and heat.

And she wanted to be his buddy.

"I'm not having a very good night," he said again, with new intensity.

"Must be in the air," Nicki replied with a half-hearted attempt at humor. The "little boy lost" look on his face was doing painful things to her heart. To distract herself, she slipped off her shoes, bending over her knees to stare at her cherry-red toes. "I can't feel them. My feet are two blocks of ice. Look . . . I can't even wiggle my toes."

Val sighed and covered his eyes with both hands. "Take off your nylons, Squeaky."

"What?"

"Take off your nylons," he repeated, still hiding his eyes. "Your panty hose, your tights, whatever the hell you call them. Don't worry, I'm not looking. You can trust me—I'm dependable, remember?"

There was a slightly sour emphasis to the word "dependable" that didn't escape Nicki. Keeping a wary eye on him, she stood up and reached beneath her dress, peeling off her panty hose. "Are you peeking?"

He shook his head, tawny hair flying, hands still in place. "Heck, no. I'm being dependable. You decent?"

"I saw eyes between fingers."

"You have a suspicious nature, Squeaky." He dropped his hands and patted the sofa cushion. "Sit. No—with your back against the arm. That's good. Now put your feet in my lap."

She did as she was told without argument, since the blood rushing to her numb feet suddenly felt like a boiling bath. "Ouch, ouch, ouch . . . they hurt, they hurt. I have fireworks in my toes."

"We need to warm you up, to get your circulation going. Silly Squeaky, didn't anyone ever tell you not to wear evening shoes if you're going to play in the snow? Stop kicking, I can't rub your feet if you kick. I'm trying to be a good Samaritan here."

Nicki groaned as the sparkling nerve chills of sensation in her feet turned to cramps that curled her toes. "I doubt I would have worn these shoes if I'd known you were going to make me walk fifty zillion miles in a . . . oh, rub harder . . . blizzard. That feels better. Don't stop. Rub harder . . . harder. Oh, that feels so *good*. . . ."

Val wasn't cold any longer. He was breaking out in a sweat, and it didn't have a thing to do with the temperature in the room. The trouble was, he had a vivid imagination. Right now he was imagining Nicki in his bed, her hair tangled wild and dark across the pillow, her blue eyes softly unfocused with heat and desire. He could feel her back arching against him, her skin slick and hot against his, her hands working convulsively over the muscles in his chest. *That feels so good . . . harder. . . .*

"So tell me something." Nicki put her head back against the cushion, regarding him from beneath half-closed lids. "Do you still eat candy bars by the dozen when you're upset about something?"

His hands continued the massage, the tips of his fingers concentrating on the sensitive underside of her feet. His dark gaze skimmed the curves of her bare legs, lingering on the hem of her dress that fanned gently around her hips. He wanted to slide his hands over her thighs, to hold her gaze with his while he slowly pushed her dress to her waist. . . .

"Whatever gave you that idea?" he asked hoarsely, wrenching his gaze to the candy wrappers on the coffee table. "I'm a big boy now. I outgrew my candy dependency a long time ago. What about you? Do you still buy chewing gum by the case?"

Her smile was dreamy as his fingers tickled circles around her toes. "Bite your tongue. I'll have you know I'm a refined and sophisticated woman. I don't chew bubble gum when I have anxiety attacks. I take Valium like all the other refined and sophisticated women."

Val sent a desperate look around the cluttered room, searching for some distraction from the lady with the smoky voice and provocative smile. He was walking on the crumbling edge of his self-control. Abruptly he lifted her feet and swung them off his lap. Not exactly a debonair move, but he truly had no idea how long his restraint would last. "That's enough. You'll be fine now." *I wish I could say the same thing about me.* "I'll go make some coffee. All I have is instant, but at least it will be hot."

He practically sprinted from the room, bulldozing his way through the swinging louvered doors to the kitchen. Nicki sat up slowly, watching the doors swinging wildly on their hinges.

She didn't understand the man. Every time she thought they had reached a point where they could be comfortable with each other, he unnerved her with another of his volatile mood swings. He'd changed so much since those days on Newton Street. He had his secrets now; there were times when she looked into his dark eyes and saw a door closing.

Is it that way with all of us as we grow up and grow old? We didn't mind sharing our fears when we were children. When do we start building the walls?

She got up and walked idly around the room,

digging her bare toes into the warm pile carpet. She was tired; exhaustion must be making her morbid. This apartment bore testimony to the fact Val Santis hadn't changed all that much. The furniture was a haphazard collection of styles and colors; nothing looked as if it had been purchased to complement anything else. Obviously he still had little interest in hearth and home. Val had always been a wanderer, making his way in life with his keen wit and his easy good humor. He'd never needed or wanted roots. He'd always been more interested in what he might find around the next corner. When she thought about it, it really wasn't surprising that he'd gone into police work. It was probably the only legitimate job that wouldn't bore him to death.

"Here you go." Val came through the kitchen doors carrying a steaming mug of coffee in his hand. His jacket was gone, and the sleeves of his dress shirt were cuffed to his elbow. "This ought to warm you up."

Nicki took the cup from him, closing her eyes and inhaling the fragrant aroma. "Mmmm, that's nice. Where's yours?"

"I had a drink in the kitchen." Specifically, a shot of whiskey for medicinal purposes. The prospect of Nicki sleeping in his bed—all by her little lonesome—was doing nasty things to his nervous system. "Poor Squeaky . . . you have circles around your pretty blue eyes big enough to swallow them. Sit tight for a minute while I straighten my bedroom and put some fresh sheets on the bed. I don't want you having nightmares tonight because of my sloppy house-keeping."

"What about you?"

"I don't have nightmares." He grinned and waggled his eyebrows at her. "Sometimes I have these incredible dreams, though—"

"Where are you going to *sleep*?"

"On the sofa. I always sleep on the sofa on New Year's Eve. It's a tradition with me."

Nicki stared at him over a cloud of steam. "Absolutely not. I won't take your bed. Find me a blanket, and I'll be just fine out here."

"*I'll* be just fine out here," Val said.

"And so will I."

Val's dark eyes brightened with boyish enthusiasm. "Whatever you say, Squeaky-pooh. I hate to argue. We'll be fine *together* on the sofa. Come to think of it, I'll probably be better than fine."

"Think again." Unruffled, she sat down on the couch, legs curled up beneath her. She took a sip of coffee before she spoke. "I've been taking care of myself for a long time now, Santisi. You can't manipulate me, no matter how adorable you are. This sofa is more my size than yours, and that's that. Could you find me an extra pillow?"

"Adorable?" Val asked. He couldn't help himself.

She smiled then, taking in his shining, disheveled hair, the dimple that came and went in his cheek, the hard elegance of his square jaw. Oh, the spells he could weave simply by breathing.

Her smile faded as she met his gaze. Those beautiful, eternal eyes . . . shining bright and dark at once, so intense and hungry, she almost gasped out loud. She could feel the way his body had altered, the tightening of his muscles, the electricity that

shivered in the space between them. They looked a
each other for a long moment, the most uncertair
moment of her life. She was conscious of a warmtl
flowing to her breasts, filling them with a tinglin;
weight. Her hips shifted slightly on the cushion.

She had to get it together. This could happen so
easily, and then she would be lost in him. She was
afraid he was going to touch her, and she didn'
know what she would do then.

Yes, she did. She knew.

She dropped her gaze. "I'm tired," she said, hei
voice coming out a little fractured. "I'd like to go to
sleep now, if you don't mind."

The message was clear. Val stepped back, shoving
a trembling hand through his hair. He couldn't seem
to breathe deeply enough to ease the tightness in his
chest. His self-control was so close to snapping, he
had no choice but to abandon chivalry. He turned
and stalked to the linen closet in the hall and pullec
out a blanket and a spare pillow, then returned to
the living room and tossed them on the sofa.

"Anything else I can get you?" he asked through
his teeth. His nerves were showing, but he didn't give
a damn.

Nicki shook her head. "This is all I need. Thanks."

"Lucky you." He turned on his heel. "You'll sleep a
hell of a lot better than I will tonight."

An hour later he was still wide awake.

It may have been because he hadn't actually lair
down on his bed. He sat there in the dark, fully
dressed, poised on the edge of the mattress like a

man expecting a fire drill. He heard the water running in the bathroom. He heard the faint sound of sofa springs creaking once or twice, then the apartment settled into silence.

He closed his eyes tight for the longest time. He could handle this. He could.

The hell he could.

He stood up. He walked to the door, then turned and walked right back to the bed and sat down again. A soft groan escaped him as he buried his head in his hands. He had no idea what he was doing. He was floundering. He was losing his objectivity. He was *dying* for her. By inches.

It was a perfect way to begin the New Year. There was absolutely nowhere to go but up.

Four

It didn't look good for the society columnist of *The Washington Observer*.

Nicki walked slowly through the lobby of her apartment building, past the security guard at the front desk, past Roy the diligent janitor who was polishing the brass light fixtures on the wall, past the silver-haired matron from the penthouse who was taking her three poodles out for their morning walk. They all stared at her, even the poodles. No one missed the slight stagger in her step. No one missed the oh-so-cautious way she held her head, or the telltale circles under her eyes. They drew their own damning conclusions, Nicki was sure . . . even the poodles.

And who could blame them? It was eight o'clock in the morning on New Year's Day, and she was slinking home wearing last night's makeup and wrinkled evening clothes. She tried to hold her head high, but it was impossible. Something had happened to her neck while she'd slept on Val's amazingly uncomfortable sofa. The muscles had seized up, pulling her head forward and to one side. It was extremely painful, and it made it difficult to see where she was going. To make matters worse, her evening shoes had changed size since her walk through the snow the night before. The delicate straps that crisscrossed her heels and ankles had stretched to useless proportions, leaving her shoes dangling on her feet. She couldn't take two steps without wobbling. No, it didn't look good.

The walk to the elevator had never seemed so long. Once the doors had closed, she had the dubious pleasure of staring at her reflection all the way to the fifth floor. Three walls of the elevator were mirrored, and Roy the diligent janitor kept them sparkling clean. It was a humbling experience. The only comfort she had was the fact that Val hadn't seen her looking and feeling so . . . Squeakyish. She had been up and out of his apartment the moment she heard the snowplows rumble by on the street below. The note she left him had been scrawled across an old envelope and slipped beneath his bedroom door: *Have your sofa exorcised—it tried to kill me. Gone home to recover. Thanks for an unforgettable New Year's Eve.*

It was impersonal and flippant, but she hadn't known what to say. She'd never before been faced with the Morning After the Night That Wasn't. There seemed no way to take her leave with aplomb.

Back in her apartment, she stripped off her clothes and treated her stiff muscles to a long, steamy shower. Afterward she donned her terry-cloth robe and curled up in bed among a mountain of pillows, hoping to catch up on her sleep. It was impossible. She tossed fitfully, frustrated and confused by the yearnings that plagued her. Something was happening to her, something she couldn't control. It echoed in her heart, bounced off the walls of her bedroom, hummed in her ears. No matter how hard she tried, there was no getting away from it.

In desperation she got up and went to her closet. She pulled a bright pink box from the top shelf, looking over her shoulder as if she expected to find someone spying on her. This was her secret stash, her addiction, her crutch when life became a little too uncertain.

Chewing gum.

She took the entire box back to her bed. Five minutes later her cheeks were bulging like a trumpet player's, and the bedspread was littered with hot-pink gum wrappers. She chewed. She chomped. She blew Olympic-size bubbles that popped one after another like firecrackers and thought gloomy and troubling thoughts.

She felt so . . . *fragile*. She was wandering in an unfamiliar emotional maze, and it didn't seem to be in her power to turn back and take a safer path. She'd been caring for herself for so long—covering all the bases, planning, learning, creating the life she wanted, right down to her name. *She* had done it, she had exhibited a resolution and resilience that had amazed even herself. It was a jolt to realize how easily her defenses could be shaken. Was emotional independence an illusion, a matter of timing? Did it all blow up in your face if you happened to encounter a certain person at a certain moment? Did it all come down to *chance*? It was a depressing thought.

One of her bubbles got away from her just then, exploding all over her nose and cheeks and chin. She rose up on her knees so she could see her reflection in the dresser mirror, scowling as she peeled off her pink mask. *He* was responsible for this. He'd put her in this pathetic condition. He'd made her uncertain and restless and discontented. She ought to be furious with him. Lord only knew why she kept glancing at the telephone through the corner of her eye.

Don't hold your breath. The number is unlisted, remember?

What is it you want, Nicki?

Hell's bells, don't think about what you want.

She threw herself backward on the bed, sticky fingers pressed over her eyes. She could see him in that secret world behind her closed lids, and what she saw overwhelmed her: his fallen-angel eyes and the hard line of his cheek and his wicked, teasing smile. The wildness. Val Santisi played life like a game; seldom serious, yet somehow more alive than anyone else she had ever known. The feelings he aroused in her were seductive and mysterious and reckless . . . just as he was.

It would be so easy, she thought.

Giving in.

Three days later, Val Santisi walked into the six-story office building that housed *The Washington Observer*. His broad shoulders gave beautiful shape to a fawn-colored suede jacket that matched exactly the lightest streaks in his wind-tossed hair. He spoke with the pretty young blonde at the reception desk, thanked her with a preoccupied, crooked smile, and proceeded to the wall of elevators. He didn't notice the way she slumped down in her seat as she stared after him, feverishly fanning herself with a manila folder.

It was late, nearly 6:00 P.M. Everyone seemed to be making a beeline for the front doors; Val expected a solitary ride to the fourth floor.

He was wrong. Boy, was he ever wrong.

She walked in at the last second. Val had to jam his foot into the elevator track to keep the doors from closing on her. Her hips cleared by an eighth of an inch.

And oh, what hips they were. Val's head swiveled on his neck as he followed her progress to the back of the elevator. She wriggled. She undulated. She swayed with a lazy, eyepopping rhythm, the rounded shape of her full buttocks cleanly and perfectly molded in the tightest, shiniest, shortest black leather skirt Val had ever seen. She wore a waist-length white fur jacket and knee-high leather boots with four-inch heels. Glossy strawberry-blond hair danced in miniature corkscrew curls halfway down her back. From the rear she was a vision of lush feminine pulchritude.

And then she turned around.

The jacket hung open, clearly revealing Mother Nature's generous bounty. Her tiger-striped V-neck sweater was tight and trembling over prodigious breasts. A silver belt with a sequined buckle the size of a hubcap hugged an incredibly tiny waist. Heavy makeup emphasized exotic green eyes, and brilliant red lipstick shimmered on her pouty Marilyn Monroe mouth.

Val couldn't remember what came after inhaling.

"Hello?" She fluttered false eyelashes at him, tipping her head sideways. "Honey, are you holdin' that door for someone?"

He shook his head, trying to wiggle his foot from the track.

"Is your *foot* stuck?" Her eyes filled with dismay, and her southern accent became more pronounced. "Lordy, is your poor foot stuck in that ol' door? Let me scoot down there and help you pull it—"

"Stay put. I've got it." Val didn't want Scarlett O'Hara bending over and becoming an instant centerfold. Face stinging with warm blood, he wrenched his foot free. The straining doors closed with an angry rumble. "Which floor would you like?"

She giggled breathlessly, as if he had made an incredibly witty remark. "Sounds like you're makin' me a present. I've never had anyone offer me a whole floor before. I believe I'd like the sixth floor, please."

"Sixth it is." He punched the button, then backed into the closest corner. The elevator lurched into motion, and she giggled again, grabbing on to the handrail. Val smiled vaguely in her direction, trying to focus on something that wasn't pink, round, or bouncy. It wasn't easy. He reached up to loosen his tie and remembered he hadn't worn one.

"Probably you can smell me," she said apologetically.

Val wondered if he'd heard right. "What?"

"Had a little trouble with my atomizer, don't you know. My perfume started squirtin' out like a fire hose. French perfume, mind you—fifty dollars an ounce, and I pretty much took a bath in it. I'm a little potent in such close quarters."

Val's eyes glinted with humor. "Yes. I mean . . . no. What I mean is . . . you're very fragrant."

"Aren't you sweet?" Her breasts rose and fell with a mesmerizing sigh. "I swear, some men would have said, 'Serena Grace, you're stinky tonight.' Some men just don't have any *finesse*, y'know? Dylan's not like that, thank goodness. He's my boyfriend. He works here. He's just about the smartest . . . well, speak of the devil himself! Dylan, honey bear!"

Somehow the elevator had reached the sixth floor without Val being aware of it. "Dylan honey bear" was framed in the open doors, a slender blond fellow with a cherubic face and a shirt pocket full of pens and pencils. This was a happy man. His eyes sparkled with pleasure behind wire-rimmed glasses as Serena Grace sashayed toward him.

"You're only five minutes late," Dylan marveled, as if Serena Grace had accomplished a remarkable feat. "This is wonderful. I was just telling Nicki how much I was looking forward to your show tonight."

A damn fine leather skirt, Val decided dreamily, trailing a few steps behind Serena Grace. Nicki would look absolutely fantastic in a skirt like that. Why, with her cute little . . .

Nicki.

Val stopped dead in his tracks. There she stood, right next to Dylan honey bear. She was wearing a rose-colored suit with a fitted jacket and a short, pleated skirt. Her dark hair was caught at the nape of her neck with a snowy white scarf. She looked vibrant, classy, adorable. He couldn't understand how he had overlooked her.

"Hey there, Squeaky." He noticed the color in her cheeks matched her dress. He also noticed her expression was about as warm as a frosted beer mug. Instinct told him to proceed cautiously. "I was in the neighborhood, so I thought maybe I'd drop in and surprise you."

"Squeaky?" Dylan echoed with relish, tearing his eyes away from Serena Grace long enough to grin at Nicki. "I could have sworn I heard the man call you *Squeaky.*"

"You must have heard the man wrong," Nicki said, her tone daring Dylan to argue with her. She wasn't feeling too friendly at the moment. She might have been a fly on the wall for all the notice Val had given her when he'd walked out of the elevator. He had been completely mesmerized by the hypnotic movements of Serena Grace's rolling derriere.

So what did Serena Grace have that she didn't have?

Majestic proportions, a warm and demonstrative nature, and a dance review called "Appointment with Ecstasy."

She met Val's gaze hoping he couldn't hear her teeth grinding. "How are you, Val? Feeling all right?"

"I'm feeling just fine," Val said. His tone was hesitant, his eyes narrowed thoughtfully. At the moment little Squeaky Boggs put him in mind of a powder keg giving off sparks. Apparently he had done something to irritate her. He wished he knew what it was.

"That's a relief," Nicki replied. "When you stepped out of the elevator with your face all flushed and blotchy, I thought you might be coming down with chicken pox or something. Well, no matter. Where are my manners? Serena Grace, Dylan Lichter—I'd like you to meet Val Santisi. We knew each other when we were growing up back in New Jersey. Of course, Val's several years older than I am."

Definitely irritated. Val shook Dylan's hand and nodded at Serena Grace, all the while keeping a wary eye on Nicki. The smile she gave him sent frosty fingers skittering down his spine. "Is this a bad time? I was hoping you'd be free for dinner, Nicki. If I've interrupted your work—"

"Not to worry, we've already put in our twelve hours for today." Dylan threw a ropy arm around Serena Grace and pulled her close. "As a matter of fact, Serena Grace and I are heading over to the Zephyr Club to grab a bite to eat before her first show. I invited Nicki to come along, but—"

"Sugar," Serena Grace interrupted, "that sharp ol' pencil in your shirt pocket is pokin' me right in the—"

"Sorry." Coloring a bright pink, Dylan dropped his arm and stepped back. "I forgot I was armed. I'll leave all pointed objects in my desk before we leave tonight. Where was I?"

"Something about Serena Grace's first show," Val put in, trying to discipline the smile that threatened. "Serena Grace, do you sing, or . . . something?"

"Can't sing a lick," she replied cheerfully. "My

God-given talent is *rhythm*, don't you know. I dance. Just give me a beat, and I start to move."

Val nodded. "I can just imagine."

At this point Nicki decided she had had quite enough. Val was drooling puddles over the voluptuous and rhythmic Serena Grace. Most men did; Val was simply reacting like most men. Unfortunately Nicki's reaction was a strong impulse to kick him in the danger zone.

"Well, don't let us keep you," she said to Dylan. "Have a lovely evening, and good luck with your show, Serena Grace."

"Have a lovely evening with us," Dylan insisted. "I know you're free tonight, Nicki—you told me this was the first Friday night since Thanksgiving you didn't have a party to attend. Convince her, Santisi. It's no fun sitting by myself while Serena Grace does her show. Women keep hitting on me. They can't help themselves, but it's damned embarrassing, and it makes my Angel Pie here absolutely furious."

Serena Grace chortled and punched him in the shoulder. "Dylan, honey, you just slay me!"

Dylan grinned proudly. "I slay her. What do you say, guys? Four for dinner? I can promise you a night to remember."

"And I do love knowing I have friends in the audience," Serena Grace added. "As an artist, I find support and encouragement invaluable to me."

"I never turn down a night to remember." Val looked at Nicki, his head tilted inquiringly to one side. His gold-and-brown hair fell about his face in glossy disarray; his smile was a question. "How about it, Squeak—uh, Nicki? Serena Grace would appreciate our encouragement and support."

Nicki stared at the paper-thin scar that nicked his eyebrow, a memento of a motorcycle accident fifteen years earlier. It made him look vulnerable, which he wasn't, and devilish, which he was. He knew she couldn't refuse without looking petty and churlish.

"I'm not exactly dressed for a nightclub," she said.

"Just take the scarf out of your hair," Serena Grace offered helpfully. "Shake your head, maybe undo a couple of buttons on your jacket . . . you know, loosen up a little. You'll look just fine, honey.

"Loosen up a little," Val murmured. His dark eyes gleamed.

Nicki forced a smile, her fingers curling into fists behind her back. "I'll do my best."

Loosening up was easier said than done, Nicki discovered. Particularly when viewing "Appointment with Ecstasy."

"This is amazing," Val whispered in Nicki's right ear. "*Glow-in-the-dark Hula-Hoops.* How can she swing them like that, every one moving in a different direction? I have never seen a woman with such . . ." A pause here. "Such coordination."

Nicki slumped a little lower in her chair, pink-cheeked and wide-eyed as Serena Grace and her Hula-Hoops swiveled and dipped to the throbbing strains of Ravel's "Bolero." The woman was indeed coordinated. She also appeared to be double-jointed.

"She has a grand time," Dylan whispered in Nicki's

left ear. "She really enjoys herself, you know? What a woman. Gosh, what a woman."

"She's remarkable," Nicki said in a suffocated voice. She fiddled with the buttons on her jacket, feeling hot and uncomfortable and dowdy. The atmosphere at the Zephyr Club was smoky and seductive, the dress code relaxed to semiscandalous. The clientele was cheerful and boisterous, whistling and applauding as Serena Grace went through her . . . rhythmic motions. Dylan was right. Serena Grace seemed to be enjoying herself immensely.

"You're awfully quiet, Squeaky," Val said, his breath tickling her right ear. "Are you all right?"

"Don't call me Squeaky," she said. "And I'm fine. Having a wonderful time."

And from the left came another enthusiastic comment from Dylan: "Do you know what I find appealing? Serena Grace is so honest, so *comfortable* with her femininity. That's rare for women in this world today."

Nicki understood what he was saying with more clarity than she would have liked. Serena Grace was no rocket scientist, but she radiated a cheerful self-acceptance that Nicki had never quite managed to achieve. No matter how many fashionable places she frequented, how many glittering parties she attended, she was always striving to be something more than she was. More intelligent, more successful, more secure. What she *was* was never quite good enough.

You could take the girl out of the fish market. . . .

"I could use a drink," she said suddenly. Her first of the evening, and long overdue. It was high time she started loosening up. "Do you see a waitress around, Dylan?"

Dylan sighed, never taking his eyes from the stage. "Truly impressive, don't you think, Santisi? What a woman. What a performance."

Val nodded. "I've never seen anything quite like it."

Nicki excused herself and went to the bar, quite sure neither Dylan nor Val would notice her absence. She ordered something called an Injun Joe and drank it standing up at the bar. It tasted like a strawberry soda, very cold and refreshing, but without much of a kick. She was still wound as tight as a watch spring. The stiff neck she had suffered from since sleeping on Val's sofa was burning with new life, creating a demon throbbing under her skull. She rummaged through her purse until her fingers closed around a bottle of aspirin. She shook out a couple of pills and started to ask the bartender for a glass of water, then changed her mind and ordered another Injun Joe. As tense as she was two little drinks wouldn't do more than take the edge off her nerves. . . .

Ten minutes later she returned to the table. Serena Grace had just finished the second half of her act and was waving and throwing kisses from the stage. Nicki was feeling much more *simpática* with the smiling redhead; she gave her two thumbs up and a bright-eyed grin.

"She wears a feather boa well," she told Val as she sat down. "Not everyone looks good in feathers, you know. And she was very creative, don't you think? The way she used clothes as accessories and accessories as clothes . . . very original. Where's Dylan?"

"Here," Dylan said, tapping her left shoulder. "Right where I've always been. Where did you go? Are you okay?"

"Of course." Nicki propped her elbow on the table and her chin on her hand. "Much better. Much, much better. You know, I took some dancing lessons when I first came to Washington. I had a pretty good sense of rhythm myself. I think I could give Serena Grace a run for her money."

Val stared at her for a long moment. Then, with a sigh: "How many have you had, Squeaky?"

She turned her neck experimentally, pleased to find her muscles had loosened right up. "Hmmm? How many what?"

"There's something wrong here," Dylan said slowly. "She planted her elbow in my cheesecake."

He spoke the truth, Nicki realized. Her elbow was smack-dab in the middle of his cheesecake. Funny. She hadn't felt a thing. "Buggers," she said, wiping her elbow with a napkin. "I'm terribly sorry, Dylan. I'll order you another."

Val and Dylan exchanged a meaningful glance. "She was only gone ten minutes," Val said. "How much can one small person drink in ten minutes?"

"I'm not drunk," Nicki retorted indignantly. "I've never been drunk in my life. I'm always in control. In my line of work I would never risk making a spectacle of myself. I had two strawberry sodas and a couple of aspirin."

"They don't serve strawberry sodas here," Dylan said.

Nicki snorted inelegantly. "Well, they don't *call* it a

soda. It's called an Injun Joe. They're good; you should try one."

Dylan groaned and dropped his forehead into his hands. "Oh, Lord. No wonder she's ready to swing her Hula-Hoops. Nicki, there's a reason that drink is called an Injun Joe—it *sneaks up* on you. Get it?"

"Got it," Nicki said. "If Serena Grace swings her Hula-Hoops, she's coordinated. If Squeaky Boggs wants to swing *her* Hula-Hoops, she must be drunk. Right?"

Dylan shook his head as if he were clearing water out of his ears. "I keep hearing this 'Squeaky' thing. Squeaky who?"

"It occurs to me," Val put in mildly, "that this would be a good time to call it a night. Dylan, please tell Serena Grace how much we enjoyed her performance. You were right. It was an unforgettable evening." He stood, attempting to pull Nicki's chair back. "Honey, let go of the table."

"Let go of my chair." She glared over her shoulder at him. "I'm just as capable of stimulating you as Serena Grace is, and I don't have to be drunk to do it. You're being very insulting."

"I'm not," he replied earnestly, gently prying her fingers from the edge of the table. "I would never do such a thing. I know you're capable of just about anything. Why, remember all the fun we had at your place on Christmas Eve?"

"Christmas Eve?" Nicki thought about that for a moment then her face fell tragically. It may have been Injun Joe sneaking up on her, but suddenly she felt deeply remorseful. "I attacked you. I knocked you out. I tied you up."

"*Well.*" Dylan sat up attentively. "That sounds very stimulating to me."

"You have no idea." A slow smile curved Val's lips as he urged Nicki to her feet. "Say good night, honey."

He looked so tender and appealing, with a boyish crinkle of smile lines at the corners of his eyes and his honeyed-brown hair drifting about his dark face. Nicki could hardly take her eyes off him as she gave a limp-wristed wave in Dylan's direction. "G'night, honey."

Five

"Why don't we ever go anywhere in your car?" Nicki asked, watching huge lacy snowflakes settle on the windshield. She'd never seen a winter quite like this in Washington, one storm following another. "I always drive."

"You're not driving, pumpkin," Val said gently. "I'm driving. Arrive alive, I always say."

She shrugged, leaning her head against the window. The cold glass felt good to her flushed skin. "But you're driving *my* car. You never seem to bring your car anywhere. Either we walk or we take my car. I think you love me for my car." She hadn't meant to say that. The word "love," spoken aloud in the presence of Val Santisi, intensified the odd tension that shivered in the air between them. She was grateful for the darkness that hid her embarrassment. What was happening to her? She'd never been this sensitive before. She slanted Val a heavy-lidded glance, studying the stark beauty of his profile haloed in the apricot light from the dash. Her eyes settled on the sweet, sexy curves of his mouth, and her throat grew tight with longing. She felt like a starved woman who was being tempted by a delicious sinfully rich dessert.

He was more provocative, more appealing, more sensual, than any man she had ever known. When she let down her guard and allowed her mind and her body to respond, the frantic excitement inside her was almost painful.

"Looks like tonight's going to be my big chance," Val said huskily, staring straight ahead.

Her throat was so dry, she couldn't swallow. "What are you talking about?"

His shimmering liquid eyes flicked in her direction for a stinging second. "Self-control. The odds aren't very good, but I hear there's a first time for everything."

It took a moment for that to sink in. He *knew*, she realized. Everything she had been thinking, everything she had been feeling. She thought about pretending that she didn't understand him, but knew it would be futile. "You're unbelievable," she said hoarsely. "Do you honestly think the decision is up to you."

His voice was soft with amusement. "Tonight it is."

She squeezed her eyes shut tight and hugged the door, trying to slow her crazy heart.

By the time they reached her apartment, she was feeling much better. *Much* better. Her body was weightless. The apprehension and anticipation that had tormented her throughout the ride home had magically melted away. Everything would be fine. Now, as always, she was totally in command of the situation. A woman of the world who was secure enough to admit what she wanted and refused to feel guilty because of it. Totally in command.

But she couldn't get her purse open.

"What are you doing?" Val asked, rocking up and down on the balls of his feet as they stood in front of her door.

"Trying to get my key. I'm just having a little . . . problem . . . with the snap."

"It's a *zipper*," Val replied.

And so it was. Shaking her head, Nicki pulled the zipper and immediately dumped the entire contents of her bag on the floor. "Now, how on earth did that happen?" she asked, her voice detached and languorous. "I must have been holding it sideways."

Val became motionless, staring at the indistinct focus of her blue eyes. This time he saw clearly what he had missed earlier in the shadows of the car. This was something more than two sneaky strawberry sodas. He took her face in his hands, frowning down at her. "Lady, what are you *on*?"

His touch sent unexpected currents of pleasure through her. "You have beautiful lips," Nicki said, devouring him with her shrouded gaze.

"Good grief." Val blinked at her, then made a muffled sound deep in his throat and took her purse from her hands. He went down on his knees, scooping up handfuls of woman things—lipstick, perfume, wallet, a pair of earrings, two bottles of pills. . . .

Two bottles of pills. He stood up slowly, balancing both in the palm of his hand. "You said you took a couple of aspirin?" he asked Nicki.

She nodded solemnly, her smoky gaze still fixed on his lips.

"You're sure?" he persisted. "There are two different kinds of pills in your purse—aspirin and some sort of prescription."

"Muscle relaxants," Nicki said. Somehow her cheek found his shoulder, rubbing against the soft suede jacket like a cuddly kitten. "The doctor gave them to me when I kinked my neck sleeping on your sofa. Mmmm, I love your coat." She lifted her chin and put her lips close to his ear. "Let's go inside now."

Val breathed deeply, holding himself in check. It wasn't easy—Nicki's body was fusing against his in slow, sexy inches, knee to knee, hip to hip, breast to breast. She was warm, soft, and yielding; he was tense, rigid, and self-conscious.

He stepped back, awkwardly and abruptly. A small step for mankind, but a heroic and unprecedented move for Val Santisi. "You don't act like someone who has had a couple of aspirins with an Injun Joe chaser. Is it possible you accidentally took the wrong pills? The Zephyr Club was practically pitch-black—"

"No." Her slow, sweet smile shook his self-control to the core. "I don't *ever* do things like that. I'm very good at taking care of myself."

"That's very reassuring," Val muttered, staring at her dilated pupils. And what a crock, he added silently. She was more relaxed than a strand of overcooked spaghetti. He dropped both bottles of pills back into her purse, then rummaged about until he came up with her key ring. "Hold this," he ordered, slipping the strap of the bag over her shoulder. He unlocked the door, stepping aside while Nicki walked past him with a creamy smile and a pat on the cheek. "My hero," she said.

The brief touch felt much too good. Val closed his eyes and counted to ten before following her slowly into the apartment. *Don't do this,* he wanted to warn her. *Don't tempt me. I'm nobody's hero, least of all yours.*

"Don't turn on the light." Nicki was a shadowy figure standing in front of a long picture window. "I like it dark in here. It makes the city lights look so much brighter, like you could reach out and scoop them up in your hands. Come and look."

"No. I'm afraid of heights." Val went methodically from lamp to lamp, flooding every corner of the room with light. Harsh, clear, one-hundred-watt light to dispel any romantic notions he or anyone else in the immediate vicinity might have. "I'm afraid of the dark too. This is much better."

She turned, shading her eyes against the light. "What's the matter with you? You're not acting like yourself."

"Of course I'm acting like myself. There's no other way I can act." Van ran out of lamps to turn on. He stood in the center of the room, hands pushed deep in the pockets of his jacket. "Matter of fact, that's my whole trouble," he added, lowering his voice to an inaudible mutter.

Nicki kicked off her shoes, shrugged out of her coat, and let her purse drop off her shoulder, letting everything fall where it may. Then she pulled off the scarf at the nape of her neck, shaking her dark hair free. "That feels so much better. Would you like a drink or some coffee or something?"

"It's late," Val said huskily. "I need to go home." But his feet remained rooted to the floor.

She tipped her head sideways, staring at him with a curious, silent watchfulness. Then, softly: "Why do you need to go home?"

A terrifying question. She looked heartbreakingly beautiful to him, all tousled and solemn and dewy-eyed. Squeaky Boggs, grown up with a vengeance and come to haunt him for his crimes. He had resigned himself to an extremely frustrating relationship—one of tantalizing torment and unfulfilled desire. Under the circumstances, he had no choice. The problem was, he had given himself too much credit. He should have known from the beginning he wasn't capable of carrying out any great acts of selflessness when he felt like this.

A new expression came into his eyes, something close to pain, and he turned his back to her. With sudden ferocity he said, "If you were as good at taking care of yourself as you claim, you'd bloody well tell me to go home."

"You're talking as if you're my enemy. You're my friend, Val."

Her voice was close, and coming closer. He felt her hand on his back, and his eyes fell shut, his breathing coming in hard catches. It was time to say good night and walk away. Past time.

Instead he heard himself say, "You don't know

what I am. It's been thirteen years. You don't know me."

Her palm slid down the sleeve of his jacket, her fingers intertwining with his. Both hands—his and hers—were shaking badly. Nicki stared at his wide, strong back, his shoulders, at the beautiful streaky mane of hair that covered his collar. She couldn't remember the last time she had felt so completely in touch with her feelings. It was all so clear to her. She didn't want him to go away. She wanted him close to her.

She put her chin on his shoulder, staring straight ahead at the same white wall he seemed to find so fascinating. "I want to know you."

He could feel the soft lineup of her body against his back and hips. Every inch. The physical response was immediate—the muscles in his thighs tightened, energy surged low in his groin, his heart kicked into a hard, frantic rhythm. He wanted to turn on his heel and drag her into his arms and give her a crystal-clear introduction to the man she called a friend. He wanted to brand every inch of her, to possess her inside and out until he relieved the painful, insistent throb deep within him. He wanted her *now*, and he wanted her on his terms, and he knew she wouldn't stop him.

He looked down at the small hand curled so confidingly into his. For a second his vision blurred, and he almost laughed aloud. It was the closest he had come to anything resembling tears since breaking his arm in the second grade. And why? He really didn't know. If he had the soul of a poet, which he

idn't, he might have said his heart was breaking. Or
erhaps—and this was more in keeping with his
haracter—the consequences of the noble act he was
ontemplating was moving him to tears.

"If you have a tape recorder, you might want to
urn it on." He squeezed her hand once, probably
uch too tightly, then disengaged his fingers from
ers. "I'm about to betray a lifelong code of question-
ble ethics. I probably won't believe it myself unless
's played back to me."

Nicki could feel the change in his body, a determi-
ation and rigidity that seemed to put him a thou-
and miles away from her. She gave a little sigh and
tepped back. "What are you talking about?"

He could do this, Val told himself. Count to three
nd turn around, and for once in his life take the
onorable and totally frustrating way out. It would
e reinforcement for his moral fiber.

"Friends look out for each other, Squeaky." When
e faced her, he had a smile of sorts in place, and his
eavy lids shuttered the hungry light in his eyes. "Or
o I've heard. You don't know what you want tonight.
o for now . . . we'll leave it be."

Nicki stared at him, watching the muscle that
orked in his brown cheek. Whatever his words
aid, he was hurting for her, and there was an
nfamiliar, primitive satisfaction in knowing that.
Ie was the one who knew all the moves, who took all
he risks. She was the one who had spent a lifetime
enying her needs in favor of security, yet there they
vere with the roles suddenly reversed. The lamb was
howing a dangerously reckless streak, and the lion
lidn't know what to make of it.

He was wrong about one thing, though. She knew exactly what she wanted tonight. She told him so now with her eyes, with her soft, slow smile. She wasn't about to "leave it be."

"Dammit," Val said, watching her. His gaze dropped to her lips and held there. "Dammit," he said again softly.

She shook her head and took a step toward him. "Don't be damning anything, Santisi. That's tempting fate. You should take what comes your way and make the most of it. Be grateful for it."

"I don't believe in fate." His hands had a will of their own. He reached up and tangled his fingers in her hair, pushing it away from her face. "I make my own fate."

She tipped back her head, staring up at him with dreamy, half-closed eyes. Her back arched slowly until her hips brushed his. "Make mine," she whispered.

Something inside him shattered. It may have been the fragile hold on his self-control, it may have been his sanity. He didn't know, he didn't care. His hands slid down her back to her skirt, gathering fistfuls of fabric at her hips. He jerked her even closer to him, his stomach muscles wrenching as the hard, swollen part of him pressed against the tender part of her body.

"This was your idea," he said hoarsely, his eyes blazing. "Remember that."

His hands tightened in her hair, holding her captive. His lips hovered over hers for a split second, then a deep groan sounded in his throat as he kissed her, long and hard, drinking from her mouth with insatiable hunger. His tongue went deep, sending pleasure shocks shimmering inside her chest. Nicki's hands found his shoulders and clung there, white-knuckled and trembling. Her body came alive with a vengeance, making her feel wanton and glorious and utterly female. Her breasts throbbed with a combination of pleasure and pain, her nipples contracted, a deep ache burned to life low within her. Her mouth fell open against his as his hands tugged on her skirt, first left, then right, rocking her in the cradle of his thighs. The demanding, primitive rhythm left her weak-kneed and gasping, her hips instinctively seeking the sating hardness of muscle and sinew. Val pulled his head back slightly, his damp mouth bared against his teeth as he stared down at her. His hair was tangled over his forehead; his cheeks were taut and flushed. He was making the rules now, and his eyes dared her to stop him as his hands slid around her hips, cupping her buttocks. He lifted her off the ground as if she weighed nothing at all, pressing her back against the white stucco wall with one swift, hungry movement. Her skirt rode high on her thighs as her legs wrapped around him, drawing him against her. Nicki was all feeling and no thought, the most basic urges completely taking over her body for the first time in her life. There was an aching, writhing emptiness inside her, desperate to be filled. She couldn't get close enough to him, and she couldn't stop trying—her nails digging into his shoulders, her breasts rubbing against his chest, her femininity bruised and tormented by the throbbing pressure of his hard, warm maleness. She heard him say something and wordlessly shook her head, needing to concentrate on the deep-rooted sensations that fountained within her.

His forehead fell against hers as his hips began to thrust, and somehow the clothes between them only heightened the exquisite pleasure. The stroking motions made her damp and hot, and she began to moan softly each time he rubbed himself against her. Her body had been made for this, for him. Her legs crossed at the ankles around his waist, squeezing with convulsive movements. She needed him so. She'd been needing him all her life. Brother, friend, lover . . . in this moment, he was all that, and so much more. Absolute truth flowed through her, warm and sustaining.

"I need you," she muttered against his mouth, her shaking fingers framing his face. "I've never felt like this. I need you so much. . . ."

He barely heard her hoarse whisper. He wanted the barriers between them gone before he lost his mind. The driving motion of his hips stilled abruptly as he lowered her to the floor. Her eyes went wide in protest, and he reassured her with a labored smile. His hands went to the buttons of her jacket, opening them one by one with an impatient flick of his wrist. The deep rose fabric fell open, exposing the tantalizing thrust of her breasts beneath a flesh-colored chemise. His gaze darkened as he saw the hard thrust of her nipples between the delicate lace material. He made a wordless sound as she raised her hands, touching herself where he stared. She lifted the creamy weight of her breasts, silently offering herself.

His breathing thickened, hurting his chest and throat. She looked so willing and unguarded at that moment, so reckless. A soulmate with wild blue eyes, putting every fantasy he had ever had to shame. Waiting for him. Wanting him.

And he couldn't go through with it.

The silence became deafening. Nicki watched him, growing awareness in her eyes. Slowly she pulled her jacket around her, as if she were cold. "Val?"

"You smell like flowers," he whispered, touching the burning wing of her cheekbone. "I would have never dared to imagine someone like you wanting to be with someone like me. You're very . . . very special."

She shook her head faintly. Her hair drifted in a soft curtain over his hand. "And you're not?"

"We're not talking about me. You're the one who needs looking after tonight."

"You're right." She turned her head, rubbing her swollen lips against his hand. "So look after me."

"Don't you understand? I'm *trying.*" His shoulders rose and fell with a hard breath. This would kill him; his newly awakened sense of chivalry would kill him. Her warm little body was nestling against him with gentle stubbornness, pushing him to the edge of his endurance. Yet he couldn't pull away. "Help me, Squeaky. This once, for you . . . I need to do the right thing."

She slipped her arms around his waist. "Does this feel wrong to you?"

"Listen." He framed her face in his palms, feeling as if he were touching something so beautiful, so

precious, he would never be capable of protecting
enough. His eyes held hers for a long, despera
moment. "Please . . . just listen to me. I want yc
to go in your bedroom and lock the bloody door ar
go to sleep."

"Lock the . . . ?"

"All right, I'm not giving myself enough credit. Ju
close the damn door . . . tight." He had too muc
pride to tell her he doubted his ability to control h
hunger, no matter what his conscience dictated.
don't want to hurt you, Squeaky."

"What do you think you're protecting me from"
Nicki asked painfully. "I'm all grown up now, Val.
make my own decisions. The last thing I need is
savior."

He made a frustrated sound in answer, then move
suddenly, propelling her from him. "Well, you've g
yourself one anyway," he said flatly. He turned awa
and walked to the window, deliberately keeping h
back to Nicki.

"Val?" Nicki whispered.

Don't touch me, don't come any closer. "Go to bec
Squeaky. I'll let myself out. We'll talk tomorroy
when we're both thinking straight. There are son
things you need to know."

For a moment he wasn't sure what she would d
He held his breath, his jaw set, his hands balled int
fists.

"I don't think I like you very much right now," sh
said, quite clearly.

Val heard the rustle of her clothing as she left th
room, winced at the sound of her bedroom doc

losing—*tight*. Then his head fell back, and he closed his eyes. He hadn't thought it would leave him feeling so empty and alone, this belated, noble stand he had taken.

"Funny." His quiet voice was webbed with strain. "I don't like myself very much, either."

Six

He couldn't go home. The restlessness inside him was more explosive than anything he had ever felt. He walked the streets in the dark and cold, not thinking at all. Just moving, putting one foot in front of the other, smiling a little when a couple of drunks emerged from a bar and began following him. He would enjoy expending a little of the energy that was eating him alive. But when he turned and waited for them on the sidewalk, they had a change of heart and crossed the street. Pity. If he was going to find any action, he'd have to look elsewhere.

And he knew just where to look. He walked to Military Heights, an exclusive residential area where elegant town houses grew tall and close together, chained with decorative wrought-iron gates. It didn't take him long to locate the right house, a redbrick Georgian mansion with lights ablaze. Cars were parked along both sides of the street for two blocks

n either direction. It was quite a party, still going
strong at one in the morning.

He waited behind a shadow wall of snow-frosted
evergreens, studying the iron fretwork that decorated every window on the second and third stories.
It might have been designed specifically for climbing
up . . . or climbing down.

With a little bit of luck it could turn out to be a very
satisfying evening after all.

Nicki woke with a faint start. A hungry, aching
warmth pulsated between her legs, bringing back
her dreams with shameful clarity. Her nightgown
was tangled around her hips, invisible currents
running to the peaks of her softly swollen breasts.
She groaned deep in her throat, arching her back,
pressing her hands over her mouth. Her body felt
bruised, almost painfully sensitive and tender. It
was unbearable, having him touch her so intimately
in her sleep, drawing her to the very edge of something she wanted so badly . . . then waking to find
herself alone. Resentful. Embarrassed. Unsatisfied.

What would it have been like to have him with
her? To watch him sleeping beside her, to have all
the time in the world to memorize the texture of his
skin, the softness of his hair, the curve of sweetly
shaped muscle . . .

Oh, Val. What have you done to me?

The soft colors of dawn were lighting her room. She
pulled on a robe and went to the kitchen, fixing herself a strong cup of coffee that would probably irritate
an already bad case of nerves. When she went back

through the living room holding the steaming mug in both hands, Val was sitting on the sofa. Strangely enough, his presence didn't startle her at all. She wondered if she'd known all along he would come back.

His hair was sparkling with frost, his cheeks burned raw from the cold. He was looking down at his hands, rubbing them briskly together, but she knew all his attention was focused on her. Nicki's pulse began softly pounding, pounding.

"You look frozen," she said huskily. "Are you all right?"

"I'm fine." He lifted his head long enough to give her a faint smile. "Just thawing out. I think I went a little farther than I should have tonight."

Elaborately calm on the outside, alarmingly sensitive on the inside, she walked over to him and pressed the coffee mug into his hands. "Here, this should help. You took a walk? For five hours?"

"Thank you." He sipped the coffee, his expression carefully devoid of emotion. Yet for all his quiet demeanor, the air around him seemed to live and breathe, crackling with a barely controlled tension. "I shouldn't be here. I should have gone home. I meant to."

"Did you?" Her voice was less than a whisper.

He looked up. He held her gaze for the longest time, then took a deep breath and set the coffee cup on a glass end table. He rose and walked across the room to an antique curio cabinet where a collection of crystal figurines was displayed. Rose-colored sunlight filtered through plantation shutters, tinting Val's skin and hair with a rainbow of color. He opened the cabinet door, took out a delicate figurine, and held it up to the light. "Beautiful things," he said in a husky, mesmerizing voice. "Valuable things, precious things . . . they're hard to come by. Believe me, I know. Yet look at you . . . in a few short years you've surrounded yourself with the best life has to offer. You're an amazing woman, Squeaky."

She shook her head, trying to identify the unfamiliar tone in his voice. "There's nothing amazing about me. I have a good investment counselor, a strict budget, and a generous expense account. I just need to be . . . secure, that's all."

"You're not giving yourself enough credit." His mouth quirked in a parody of a smile. He replaced the figurine, closing the glass door with meticulous care. "You've become everything you set out to be, while I . . . well, let's just say this *becoming* has been more complicated than I expected."

"How can you say that?" Nicki asked. "The work you do, the people you help—"

"I think I love you," Val said.

Nicki's fingernails cut deep into her palms. She barely felt the pain. She held her breath as their gazes locked again. Words were beyond her; a hard shiver racked her body.

"Say something." He lifted and dropped his hand in an awkward gesture. His face darkened with hot color. "Send me to the devil or let me down easy or pour out your heart, but . . . say *something*."

Still she couldn't speak. She could only stare at him, frantically committing the moment to memory— the defenseless curve of his beautiful mouth, the sexual tension in his body, and the compelling emotion in his beautiful dark eyes. Tears blurred her vision.

"I guess six o'clock in the morning is a bad time for true confessions," Val said flatly. He told himself he couldn't blame Nicki for retreating into embarrassed silence. She was thinking clearly now; in the sober light of morning she must have realized Val Santisi was no Prince Charming after all. Bright girl. "Don't worry about it. We'll just forget I said anything, all right? I'll go."

But when he started for the door, she lunged after him tugging on the back of his jacket with both hands. "Wait! Hold it! You're not going anywhere. I don't want you to leave. I don't care what time it is, and I don't want to forget what you said. You took me by surprise, that's all. Will you *stop*?"

"*Now* she talks," he muttered. But his heart was doing uncomfortable things in his chest, leapfrogging and tumbling and dipping. Embarrassing, unmanly things. He turned and lifted his chin, trying not to look as vulnerable as he felt. "Consider me stopped," he said.

Nicki shook her head, a slow, trembling smile spreading over her lips. Glorious realization struck. He loved her. This beautiful, sweet man with the sulky expression and a world of fierce emotion in his tired brown eyes loved her.

Softly she said, "Can't you . . . ?"

He was utterly still. "What? Can't I . . . ?"

"Can't you . . . ?"

Val rolled his eyes, his jaw clenched. "Take your time. Don't mind me, I'm just dying by inches. Can't I *what*?"

Nicki moved closer, her expression rapt as she gazed up at him. "Can't you see what you mean to me? Look at me, look in my eyes. What do you want from me? You can have anything. Don't you know that?"

Val's lips parted soundlessly. There was hope in his face, as well as quiet shock. He really hadn't expected this. Miracles were few and far between in his world. Even temporary miracles. The truth still had to be told, but in this moment, he allowed himself to feel only gratitude and love. He couldn't endure a lifetime of never knowing what it would be like to be a part of her. He needed this too much.

Hoarsely he said, "I almost believe you. I almost believe this is really happening to me."

Nicki took his hand, her fingers interlacing with his. She realized that Val Santisi truly didn't understand how remarkable he was. After all the swagger and dash, after all the adventures and the achievements and the daring gambles he'd managed to carry off, he still seemed to question his self-worth. She didn't understand why. She'd never known anyone like him.

"How could I *not* love you?" she asked earnestly.

Val closed his eyes. How could she not love him? He was perfectly capable of answering that question, but he wouldn't. Not yet. First he wanted to live out this dream.

He focused on the tips of her small fingers against his palm. They were barely visible beneath the too-long sleeves of her chenille robe. The garment was more Squeaky Boggs than Nicki Sharman; it was shapeless and worn, an unbecoming shade of green.

It looked at least ten years old, just the sort of thing she would cuddle up in if she needed comforting. He adored it. He adored her.

"I want to be with you today." His hand tightened on hers. "I need to be with you, but . . . somewhere else. Not here in your apartment, not even in this city. It's hard to explain, but . . ."

"Then don't explain." Nicki thought she understood. Val seemed to regard her high-profile lifestyle in Washington as proof that she had achieved more, *become* more, than he had. He couldn't be more wrong, but she needed time to convince him of that. "I don't care where we go. Just take me"—she drew in a shaky breath as her eyes focused on his mouth— "anywhere."

"Yes." The soft word was an erotic promise from a man who knew he could deliver. His whole body was hot and ready for her; the hunger inside him was so powerful and deep, it became something close to agony. He broke the clasp of their hands, a hard rasp of air between his teeth. "I'm going home to get cleaned up. I'll come back and pick you up in an hour. No, less than that. Forty-five minutes."

"That's an awfully long time," Nicki said wistfully.

He leveled a devastating look at her. His dark eyes smoldered, his mouth tipped in a seductive curve. "Some things are worth waiting for. Look at me. I waited thirteen years for you."

They left Washington heading west. For the first time Val drove his own car—or rather, a rental car from U-Drive-Us. When Nicki asked why, Val hesitated, then replied that his car was in the shop.

"So what kind of car does a police detective drive?" Nicki asked, happily drinking in the stark beauty of Val's profile.

"Whatever a grossly underpaid police detective can afford," Val replied shortly. "Look . . . the clouds are breaking up. We're actually going to have a sunny afternoon for a change."

Nicki had a sneaking suspicion he was trying to change the subject, but she let it go. The day was going to be perfect. She intended to be so attentive, so sweet, so adoring, that this man she loved would finally understand how spectacular he really was.

This man she loved. He wore a soft, cream-colored sweater that contrasted beautifully with his dark complexion. His remarkable hair shimmered with color and life, gold and ivory, sunlight and shadow. She could hardly take her eyes off him as they traveled the winding country roads. As a matter of fact, she didn't take her eyes off him, until he told her in a suffocated voice that she was embarrassing him to death and to please look somewhere else for a while.

Aiming to please—and sneaking only the occasional longing glance at Val—Nicki turned her attention to their surroundings. She had no idea where they were at this point, but it looked like a scene from a Currier & Ives Christmas card. The two-lane road curved and dipped through the hillocks and knolls of a picturesque farming community. Two-story clapboard houses were meticulously kept, snow-frosted fences ran straight and true, even the metal silos seemed to shine. They drove slowly as the homes grew closer together and nearer the road. They rumbled over a covered bridge, passed a small park where children bundled into shapeless snowsuits played on a gentle sledding hill. Adjacent to the park, an elegant fieldstone colonial stood far back from the road. A wooden sign hung from a brass lightpost just inside a low rock wall—THE SNOWED INN, FOOD AND LODGING.

"We're in luck," Val announced cheerfully, turning the car through the open gateposts. "A restaurant. I haven't eaten since last night, and I'm starving. How do you feel about some lunch?"

Nicki hadn't been thinking of food at all, but still aiming to please, she smiled and tried to look enthusiastic. "I'm not actually starving, but . . . you know me. I can always eat."

"Terrific. We'll have a nice relaxing lunch, then . . . then just kind of take things from there."

Lunch was anything but relaxing.

Val wasn't sure when everything started to go wrong. It may have been when the waitress seated them at a genuine antique trestle table in the big country dining room. Table and bench were made from log slabs and held together with wooden pegs. Very charming, but the bench gave him a hell of a sliver in his rear end. It would have been unmanly to cry out, so he excused himself politely and walked to the rest room. There he practically stood on his head in a totally unnatural position while he performed a lengthy surgery on himself. By the time he returned o the table nearly twenty minutes later, his corn howder was cold, and Nicki was literally twiddling er thumbs.

From that point on, conversation was sparse and argely one-sided. Val was preoccupied, trying to ecide how to tactfully handle what he saw as a elicate situation. Contrary to the impression he'd iven Nicki, it hadn't been a sudden craving for food hat had prompted him to stop at the Snowed Inn.

It had been another sort of craving.

This was more than a restaurant . . . it was also n inn. A sign in the lobby described "cozy bed hambers, beautifully appointed with antique furni- ure and genuine feather mattresses."

A feather mattress. A cozy room with no telephone. quiet town where they would have no identity xcept as lovers. It was perfect, Val told himself. It as romantic and spontaneous.

No. She might think it was tacky, feeding her unch, then leading her straight upstairs to a room. t was the middle of the day, for Pete's sake. In Jicki's elite circle of friends this sort of thing was robably not even thought of. Well, it was probably *hought* of, but not often done.

So what if it was the middle of the day? Fate had ust presented them with a beautiful present in the hape of a genuine feather mattress. It was meant to e.

He didn't want her to think he was desperate.

Why? He *was* desperate. But he also wanted to be ensitive and romantic and maybe strive for a little ophistication. This was more than a need to take er to bed, although he desired her with an intensity he'd never felt before. He also wanted to care for her, a caring that had nothing to do with sex. He wasn't accustomed to feeling such helpless compassion. His brain was humming with conflicting signals.

So how did he suggest they check in?

Sensitively?

"Val? *Val?* Would you mind excusing me for a few minutes?"

Val literally jumped as Nicki's voice interrupted his frustrated brooding. She was standing beside the table, her head tilted thoughtfully to one side as she studied him.

"When did you get up?" he asked, blinking at her. "Are you finished with your dessert?"

She lifted an eyebrow at her empty plate. "Every last crumb. That carrot cake was the most entertaining thing that's happened to me in the last hour. I'm going to the little girls' room to freshen up. You just keep on stirring your chocolate mousse and thinking your deep thoughts."

She turned away, tossing her gleaming dark hair over one shoulder. Mute and miserable, Val watched the sway of her rounded bottom in tight white stretch pants. Her red-and-white-striped sweater emphasized her tiny waist with a wide ribbed band. Hers was a most incredible body, he thought sadly as she walked out of sight. Squeaky Boggs deserved better than carrot cake.

He looked down at the dessert bowl in front of him with a ferocious scowl. Mousse soup, thanks to a half hour of compulsive stirring. So much for sophistication, romance, and sensitivity. Which left him wondering just what it was he *did* have to offer her.

The waitress brought the check. Val lingered at the table for nearly fifteen minutes before he began to worry. Nicki should have been back long ago. He paid the bill, then went outside to the car to see if she'd decided freezing to death was preferable to being bored to death. When he didn't find her there, he went back into the lobby and questioned the manager at the front desk.

"The lovely brunette in the striped sweater." The manager bobbed his head like a dashboard puppy. "Of course I remember. Who could forget? Your wife checked in a few minutes ago. She left a key for you here at the desk. One moment."

The manager retrieved the key from an old-fashioned cubbyhole on the wall. Val took it from him because it seemed to be expected, not because he had any idea what was going on. "You're . . . sure about this?"

"Sir?"

"You're certain she was"—he paused, then finished huskily—"my wife?"

"As you can see, she signed our guest book, sir. Your wife has a rather . . . uncommon first name."

And there it was, recorded in the leather-bound register in a beautiful, extravagant hand: *Squeaky Boggs*.

Slowly he underlined her name with the tip of his finger. Remembering the little girl he'd once known. Longing for the woman she'd become. Loving them both with all his heart.

He bit his lip, turning his head to look at the winding stairway that led to the second story. She was waiting for him. And somehow he knew she was feeling everything that he was feeling.

His eyes warmed and softened with something more intimate than a smile. He pocketed the room key, then shook the manager's hand with bruising sincerity. "You have a terrific place here. The atmosphere is wonderful. I can't tell you how happy I am to be here."

The manager gave him a bemused look. "Yes well . . . I hope you and your wife enjoy your stay with us. Room twelve, left at the top of the stairs."

Hope and love tearing at him, Val took the stairs three at a time. There was no need to use the key to room twelve, after all. The door was open.

She was the only thing he saw. She was standing in front of a light-filled window, her arms crossed around her waist. Her head turned as he closed the door with a soft click. Her blue eyes shone like diamonds.

"Come and look at the view," she said. "You can see the children sledding in the park from here."

But he could only stand there in the doorway, his heart in his eyes. Never had he seen anything more beautiful than Squeaky Boggs haloed in sunlight. He wanted to let the moment unfold slowly, drinking her in with every breath. She was so precious to him.

Nicki smiled self-consciously, then turned back to the window. "You're embarrassing me to death staring like that."

"I don't mean to." He came up slowly behind her, resting his chin on the top of her head and his hands on her shoulders. His hips brushed the back of her thighs with a slight, erotic pressure. He gazed out at the winter-world below, savoring this moment of true affinity. Whatever happened the next day, next week, ten years in the future . . . he would remember *this*. Always. "I'm just trying to reassure myself that this isn't a dream. If someone wakes me up right now, I'm going to be really irritated."

"I didn't know how to do this part tactfully." Nicki's voice was unusually husky. "Getting a room, I mean. So I just . . . did it."

"I will be forever grateful." He kissed her hair, closing his eyes and inhaling her fragrance.

"Val?"

"Hmmm?" His arms crossed over hers around her waist. He held her tightly. She felt so delicate and fragile to him, but he knew better than anyone just how strong she really was. "What, my love?"

"Would you please do something for me?"

If she asked me to fly, he thought, I really think I could do it. "Anything. *Anything*."

Her smoky voice broke as she whispered almost politely, "Please make love to me. I want to belong to you today."

Val's body became rigid. Everywhere. Her sweet sincerity was enough to break his heart. His hands shook as they traveled slowly up her rib cage to her breasts. His fingers tightened there; a low sound came from deep in her throat.

"Yes," he whispered hoarsely, his lips pressed against her ear. He needed this with all his being, this magical world of love and safety they somehow created together. "Oh, yes . . ."

And then she was facing him, his hands dragging her into a deep, openmouthed kiss, his hips straining against hers. Holding her, touching her, tasting her, was everything to him. Thought expired. After so many years of manipulating and plotting and staying one step ahead of everyone else, he finally allowed himself simply to *feel*. With childlike joy. With gratitude.

They broke from the kiss clinging and gasping, staring into each other's eyes with identical expressions of fierce desire and wide-eyed wonderment. Awe changed somehow to humor; they began laughing weakly, hands touching faces, still making sure the dream was real.

"I'm so happy," Nicki said, wiping a tear from her cheek with the back of her hand. "It's just . . . I'm so happy."

His eyes were smiling, his trembling hands smoothing over her hair. "I haven't done anything yet."

"You're here. You're with me. You're loving me."

"I'm about to." Then his smile faded, his palms resting on either side of her flushed face. He stared into her eyes for the longest time, needing her so, his chest aching with it. "No," he whispered. "You're absolutely right. I've been loving you for . . . oh, it feels like forever. Whatever we're doing now, it isn't making love. We've done that already, haven't we?"

"I think we started making love on Christmas Eve," Nicki said breathlessly, a lopsided smile pressing at her cheeks. "We just didn't know it."

"The longest foreplay in history," Val muttered, touching his lips to her damp, swollen mouth. He thought back to that snow-filled night, to the emotions that had swept through him with such frightening intensity. "I knew, Squeaky. I think I knew exactly what was happening."

"Don't . . . call . . . me . . . Squeaky." She punctuated each word with a smacking kiss. "My name is Nicki Sharman."

"Squeaky Boggs signed the guest register."

"Momentary lapse." She tugged his sweater up, finding the satin hardness of his rib cage. Her hands began to wander. "If you dare call me Squeaky again in this lifetime, I will torture you until you beg for mercy."

"Squeaky . . . Squeaky . . . Squeaky . . . Squeaky . . ." Val gasped for air and laughed and shook with desire, all at once. Feelings seemed to flood into the room along with the sparkling winter sunlight, crowding him with joy. Oh, he wanted to be smooth and debonair and masterful, but his happiness kept getting in the way. The darkly brooding expertise he had perfected had served him well in the past, but the past had nothing to do with this moment. He was deluged with bright, new, demanding sensations. He didn't even try to fool himself that he was the master of the situation. He felt like a child at Christmas, increasingly astonished as each succeeding gift was presented.

Her hips nudged him backward a step, toward the bed. Her blue eyes were glowing with dreamy intensity. "I love your smile," she said huskily, tracing the curve of his lips with the edge of her fingernail. "It makes you look wicked and sexy and *bad*."

"Bad? That's good?"

"Very good. Good girls love bad boys."

He touched the tip of his tongue to the pulse at the

base of her throat. Very softly: "And are you a good girl?"

"I hope so." She gasped as his hands slid down her back, tracing the hollow of her spine, cupping and squeezing her buttocks. "I'm not . . . mmm, that feels nice . . . I'm not exactly a fountain of experience."

"Neither am I," Val said. His mouth dipped to hers for an exquisite, swirling kiss. "Not this kind of experience. Everything feels new to me. I can hardly"—his tongue followed the lush outline of her lips—"wait to see what happens next."

Nicki tipped back her head far enough to look into his face. His dark eyes were burning with love, amazement, sensuality . . . and her. She loved seeing her own reflection in his heated gaze. That meant, she thought with hazy satisfaction, that she was inside his soul.

"Let's find out," she whispered.

Another wicked bad-boy smile spread slowly to his eyes and lips, making heat flare like a sunburst on her cheeks. He picked her up in his arms as if she weighed nothing. Nicki buried her face in that wonderful spot between his shoulder and jaw while he carried her to the bed, setting her gently on the edge of the mattress. She'd never felt such a bed . . . her hands sank deep on either side of her hips into the downy softness. Her eyes smiled up at Val, her parted lips shimmering wetly.

"I'm not good with words," Val said quietly, staring down at the picture she made. "But I want you to know . . . I cherish you. I want you to know that, I want you to believe it."

"I do." She loved the naked honesty in his face, the touching vulnerability. She loved his sun-streaked hair and the flush of sexual arousal on his brown skin. *I love this man*, she thought as he slowly knelt in front of her. *All my life, I will love this man.*

He took her hands in his, kissing each palm, then curved his arms around her waist and rested his head in her lap. Her hands stroked his hair, loving and gentle. Time pooled softly in the sunlit corners of the room, a timeless moment of acceptance and belonging that Val wished could last forever.

"I love you." His voice was a quiet whisper. He raised his head, and she could see that his face was filled with sweetness, as well as passion.

Nicki touched the back of her hand to his face. A smile hovered, shaky with emotion. "I love you too."

They were both smiling then, and their kiss didn't fit together properly. But smiles changed to sighs, mouths softened and parted. A growing sensation of heat shimmered between them, building in and around and between the kissing. Nicki began to pant, softly and rhythmically, her breathing matching the drumbeat in her blood.

I love this man.

Val pulled back, watching and loving the startled look in her eyes. He knew what she was feeling, because he felt it too. The aliveness. The hunger. The thrill of discovery. He reached out with unsteady hands, rolling up her sweater above her breasts. Like a child being undressed for bed, Nicki lifted her hands high as he pulled it over her head. Her bra followed, sailing over Val's shoulder to land in a square of sunlight near the window. Bare breasts jutting forward, Nicki stretched and slowly arched her back. There was no embarrassment or constraint as they held each other's gaze. They were moving from their private lives to a place new and unfamiliar, and there was a wonderful exhilaration in the unfamiliar.

With mind-obliterating shock, Val's mouth found first one breast, then the other, suckling, licking, tugging, until the triangular current from her nipples to her brain to her groin glowed white-hot. His hands spanned her slim torso, his thumbs rubbing in shaken circles over bare skin. Her womb contracted. There was a subtle swelling of her inner flesh; her head fell back weakly, and her eyes fluttered closed. The urgency within her grew steadily until she was gasping aloud; still Val continued worshiping her breasts with infinite patience, pausing between kisses while he traced his fingers in circles around the swollen peaks. Pulling her out of herself. Erasing everything from her mind, infusing her body with an intimate, burning need.

When he finally stood up, the emptiness of separation pushed her close to tears. He removed his clothes quickly, standing before her in all his male beauty, sun-bronzed and golden and flamelike. Silently, her wide eyes never moving from his face, she fell back into the mattress while he removed her shoes and stockings, eased her pants over her hips. She was no more embarrassed than he had been. She felt utterly female. Sensual. *Free.*

She felt his naked body stretch full length against hers with a shock of ecstasy. He stroked her hair with heart-lifting care, gentling her, smoothing the dark strands from her face with loving kisses. Her fingers greedily searched out the beloved lines of his face: the square line of jaw, the molding of his lips, the indentation at the center of his chin. He looked so beautiful to her, so strangely defenseless.

I love this man, was all she thought as he pressed hard and hungry against her softness. There was so much for her to explore in him, so much to learn. She found her answers with her hands and her lips. In his eyes she saw what a woman was to a man who truly loved her—she was his past, his present, his future; she was the only one who could end his separateness.

He adored the lines and curves and openings of her body with sweet, fierce attention. He gave her everything he had, everything he was: his patience, his knowledge, his love. When he silently asked, she eased her legs apart for him, shaking and needy and completely submissive. He pressed carefully and tenderly into her yielding softness *slowly*, muscles bulging in his shoulders, holding back to the edge of his endurance, until his restraint suddenly shattered. He thrust himself deep and hard, a hoarse cry escaping him. Burying himself in her center, her soul. Instinctively they moved into the beautiful, ageless rhythm, swirling through flashes of neon and fire, dancing on the edge of the flames. Losing themselves in each other, yet finding a completeness neither of them had ever known before.

So perfect, so good. Nothing had ever felt so right. She was hot and wet and gasping; he was hard and full and demanding. Pleasure flirted with pain. He went deeper in her, endlessly deeper, until there was a new, unbearable demand where they were joined. Nicki's back arched with fierce desperation, her legs twining around his straining body. They moved together as one, seeking that final flowing movement that would at last release them. And then, magically, when nothing else could save or succor them, they reached a burning peak of perfect, brilliant harmony. They held it together for a timeless, powerful moment, one body, one heart, one mind. They were filled with an effortless, overwhelming joy. They were filled with life.

The room held a tremendous quiet. Nicki's face was pressed against the moist hollow of Val's throat, her spent body sculpted to his. He cradled her tenderly in his powerful arms, feeling as if he were tucking her deep into his heart. He had loved the woman in her; now he guarded the child, so dear and fragile and beloved.

He had never believed in a divine order, a higher plane of life and love, than existed on this earth.

He believed now.

Seven

It was eleven o'clock on a Sunday morning, and Nicki was up to her chin in bubbles in an old-fashioned clawfoot tub. Her muscles were pleasantly aching in the most tender and intimate places. Her lover was sleeping like a baby in the next room.

Life was so very fine.

She began to hum, not a tune, but a soft, purring expression of utter contentment. It had been twenty-one hours since Val had closed the door to their room and locked the world away. Twenty-one hours of intense passion and soul-stirring hunger. Twenty-one hours of soft smiles and sleepy hellos and warm, gentle hugs. A glorious roller-coaster ride of love and sex and friendship and caring. The most perfect twenty-one hours of her life.

Sheer happiness overwhelmed her. A tickle started way down deep inside and grew into laughter. And she couldn't seem to stop laughing, even though she knew sweet, sexy, wonderful Val had more than earned his sleep, and she shouldn't wake him up. She scooped up a handful of frothy bubbles and tossed them over her head, then gave a joyous whoop and submerged herself completely under water.

When she came up for air, she opened one eye and found sweet, sexy, wonderful Val leaning against the door frame, his arms crossed over his bare chest. He wore baby-blue boxers that rode low on his lean hips. His gold-dusted hair looked as if a tornado had just whipped through the bedroom, and one dark brow was raised in a mildly curious expression.

"Hello," he said.

Nicki pursed her lips and blew bubbles out of her eyes. A fat strand of wet hair was sticking to her nose, and she peeled it away. "Good morning, honey pie." Laughter rollicked through her voice, but she managed a fairly composed expression. "Was I making too much noise? Did I wake you?"

"No." He came into the room, sitting Indian-style on the plush blue bath mat. He propped his arms on the edge of the tub and his softly bearded chin on his hands. "Your absence woke me. The bed was empty, and my feet were cold and my arms didn't have anything to hold on to. It was very sad. Were you trying to drown yourself? Was I that bad yesterday? And last night? And this morning?"

"No, no, no, and no." Nicki leaned her head against the back of the tub, one side of her mouth tucked up in a smile. She loved waking up to him. She loved the creases of sleep on his cheeks and the drowsy light in his eyes. She loved the sensual play of beautiful muscles when he moved and the matted triangle of gold hair on his chest. He was perfect, her lover of twenty-one hours. Down to and including . . .

"You have a hickey on your neck," she said with satisfaction.

"I don't know how that could have happened." He dangled his fingers into the bathwater, idly flicking at bubbles. "I think maybe I was ravished last night. That would account for my sore . . . parts."

"Poor baby." Her eyes danced for him as she lifted a dripping bare leg, plugging the faucet with her big toe. "No wonder you look so frail and exhausted. You must not have a great deal of stamina."

He fixed her with a dark look. "You must not have a very good memory."

"There's nothing wrong with my memory." Her amusement faded. She raised her hand, her wet finger tracing his lips. "I remember everything. The way you loved me can never be undone. It will always be a part of me."

Val shook his head, smiling faintly. "I wish I had your gift for words. When I look at you, when I'm feeling so much . . . it's all I can do to manage a simple 'hello.'"

She sat up slowly, gazing into his eyes. "Words don't matter. You don't love someone with words."

He opened his mouth to answer, then closed it again as a new feeling of helplessness swept over him. Her breasts seemed to be floating on top of the water, warm and full and wet. Her nipples were taut and perfectly round, the color of pink roses after rain. He wanted his mouth there.

"I think you're clean now," he muttered. "Would you like me to get you a towel?"

"No." Her husky little voice was luscious . . . and determined. "I want you to get in with me."

He actually watched her nipples contract, rising up tight and hard. He swallowed painfully. "Not on your sweet life. I'd drown us both and accomplish nothing else."

"We could try a little experiment. . . ."

"No, baby. I may not have all the right words to love you, but I can damn well manage all the right moves. In a *bed*, not a Squeaky-size Victorian bathtub."

Her face fell. Gently she smoothed a mound of bubbles from the curve of her breast. "You don't want to be wet with me? It wouldn't be ladylike to argue, but I think you're passing up the experience of a lifetime. I'm double-jointed, did you know?"

Val clenched his teeth. Oh, how he wanted to catch her face in his hands and invade her mouth with his tongue, to fondle and caress those rosy breasts until she was wild. Unfortunately there was a small porcelain tub standing between them, and he knew what was and what was not possible. He was also fighting an overwhelming hunger that was all out of proportion to the satisfaction he had so recently—and so frequently—received. One touch, and he thought he might explode before he ever got her to the bed. "Out," he said hoarsely. Then, with a tight, apologetic smile: "Please, Squeaky. Be good."

"All right. I was just trying to be a little creative. I don't want . . ." Her face changed, growing pink. "Well, for heaven's sake."

"For heaven's sake what?"

"My toe. It's stuck in the faucet." She looked sideways at him, biting down on her lip. "I'm not kidding. I'm really not kidding."

"Hell, woman . . ." Sexual frustration shivered through Val's deep voice. There was barely enough room on either side of the tub for Val to straddle it. He pulled, wiggled, and tugged, but Nicki's toe seemed well and truly stuck. "Maybe some soap would loosen it up."

"What a good idea." Nicki slipped down to her chin in the water with a dreamy sigh. The view from where she sat was engrossing: Val's strong brown back rippling with sinews and hollows, his tight, rounded bottom doing marvelous things for a humble pair of blue boxers. "You're just the sort of man a woman looks to in a crisis."

Something in her voice made Val look over his shoulder. His mind could not quite accept the bright-eyed innocence blinking up at him. It wasn't . . . Squeakyish. His lips slowly parted.

"You little devil," he said flatly.

Wiggling her eyebrows at him, Nicki pulled her toe from the faucet with a faint pop. Val saw the intention in her face and tried to swing his leg over the tub, but he was too late. Her arms were around his waist, tugging him backward until he lost his precarious balance. He sat down in her lap in a tidal wave of water and bubbles.

"You're . . . you're *smooshing* me!" Nicki could barely talk for laughing. There were bubbles on her eyelashes, on the floor, on the mirror halfway across the room. "And you've flooded the whole bathroom. You're in deep trouble, mister."

"Not half as much as you are, lady." Val turned over with a mighty lunge, sending a second wave of water cascading over the side of the tub. His legs crowded in between her thighs, and his chest flattened the yearning swell of her breasts. "Deep . . . deep . . ." His mouth came down hard over hers, his tongue driving deep inside. "*Trouble*," he gasped against her open lips.

"Good," Nicki whispered hoarsely. Her fingernails were on his water-slick back, following the indentation of his spine from neck to waist . . . and lower, inside the elastic band of his shorts. "The deeper . . . the better . . ."

"Shameless wench. Shameless, beautiful, gorgeous wench . . ." And then his lips were on her neck and her face and her breasts. Everything in his heart, he told her with his touch. He told her that he was going to pleasure her in every way he knew, that he was going to play with her in this too-small tub and laugh with her and rock her to her very soul, and never so much as look at another woman as long as he lived . . .

And she heard him.

Nicki cried heartbreaking alligator tears when they left the inn that evening.

When Val asked her why, she said she was afraid everything in her life would be a disappointment after this weekend. He pulled the car to the side of the road and kissed her until her body was moist and squirming and her lips were swollen and her sweater was falling off one shoulder, then asked her in a shaken voice if that was a disappointment.

"Absolutely not," she whispered, duly impressed.

The wind kicked up as soon as the sun went down, and the temperature outside dropped twenty degrees. The heater in the rental car huffed and puffed, wheezing out lukewarm air. Nicki wore only a lightweight nylon shell over her sweater, hardly enough to make up for the arctic air outside. After thirty minutes on the road she was clinging to Val like a little burr, craving his body warmth. Val stopped the car once again, pulling a face at Nicki when she gazed at him hopefully.

"Control yourself, Squeaky. We'll never get home if we keep stopping the car to make out." He pulled his black sweater jacket from the backseat and handed it to Nicki. "Here, put this on."

"What about you? You're just wearing a sweater."

"Don't worry about me," he said. "I'm a penguin. I'm used to working in the cold."

Nicki pulled on the jacket. The sleeves completely covered her hands, and she had to sit like a child while he zipped it up for her. "Stakeouts?"

A pause here. "Something like that. You look tired. Why don't you lay your head on my lap and try to sleep? It's another hour till we get back to Washington."

Nicki gave him a drowsy smile, stifling a yawn with a floppy leather sleeve. "I am tired. The very best tired I've ever felt in my life. But I don't want to sleep. Reality is only sixty minutes away. I don't want to waste any precious time sleeping."

"That's what you said last night. All night."

"And aren't you glad?" She snuggled up next to him, her head pillowed on his shoulder. "Let's talk about your work. You never tell me what you do all day. Do you always work undercover? Do you ever do nice, safe, boring things like putting on a uniform and giving traffic tickets?"

Val's gaze held steady on the road, but his jaw tightened. "It's against the law to talk about work on weekends, and we still have five hours of this weekend left. Close those baby blues, love."

"Okay, but I'm not going to sleep. I'll just adore you with my eyes shut."

He kissed the top of her head. "That's nice. No one has ever adored me before."

Sleepily: "You lie. Women started chasing after you when you were fourteen years old. I was a witness."

"But no one has ever adored me before." He took his hand off the steering wheel long enough to squeeze her fingers. "Till you, Squeaky Boggs."

"Don't . . . call . . . me . . ." She sighed, trying to remember what it was he shouldn't call her. Despite her hazy resistance, she slept almost instantly. She meandered through bits and pieces of pleasant dream images, all the while luxuriating in an incredible sensation of safety and well-being. She returned to awareness sometime later when Val gently prodded her shoulder.

"Home again," he whispered.

Nicki forced her weighted lids open. Her stuporous brain managed to register the fact they were parked in the underground terrace of her apartment building before she closed her eyes again.

"No, sweetheart. I'm taking you upstairs. You can climb in your nice warm bed and sleep the rest of the night away."

"I would adore you if you carried me."

"You already adore me, and you know it. You can walk."

Val continued promising, urging and coaxing all the way to her apartment. He unlocked the door and ushered her inside, then put his hands on her shoulders and gave her a little push in the direction of the bedroom. "G'night, angel. Sweet dreams."

Disoriented by fatigue, Nicki turned and blinked owlishly. She looked all of ten years old, with her hair tangled in her eyes and Val's leather jacket hanging to her knees. "Aren't you staying?"

"I'd like to, but I can't." Impulsively Val pulled her close, holding her tight, trying to pretend they could stay like that forever. Suddenly it felt terribly fragile to him, this brand-new bond they had forged. "Have dinner with me tomorrow night. I'll take you to a restaurant that uses real napkins. Candles on the table instead of helium balloons. Linen tablecloths. How does that sound?"

"Too good to be true." She rubbed a smile against his sweater. "What's the catch?"

"Such a witty child." Val kissed her lightly on the forehead and stepped back. There was so much to say to her, but not tonight, not when she was so tired. He wanted her to be calm and rested and . . . forgiving. "It's all part of being adorable, Squeaky. I wine you and dine you and then . . ."

Nicki grinned and tipped her head sideways. "Oh, boy. And then . . . ?"

"Then we talk," he said quietly. He could see by the curl of her lips that she thought he was teasing her. "I mean it. We need to talk. I'll call you tomorrow."

"Whatever you say." She gave him her telephone number and a wistful look. "Are you absolutely positive you want to leave me all alone tonight? What if I have a terrible nightmare?"

"Sweetheart, you haven't got the energy to have a nightmare." He allowed himself to take her face between his hands one more time, just looking at her. He stroked his thumbs across her cheeks, noticing for the first time that she had a scattering of faint freckles. Why was it always the little things that made your heart ache with emotion?

"I love you," he said, surprised at the fierceness of his own voice. "You need to know how much I love you."

He turned and left before he made a fool of himself by doing some damn fool thing like confessing his sins or taking her to bed and burying himself in her sweetness. The timing was all wrong for both. First sleep. Then the truth. Then . . .

Then what?

Nicki slept in his jacket.

She wore a cotton nightshirt, a pair of woolly socks to fight off the chill of cold sheets, and his black leather jacket. She slept soundly from eight o'clock to eight o'clock when her alarm went off. When she opened her eyes, she was up to her ears in leather and grinning like the Cheshire cat. Waking up had never, ever felt so good. And a few miles away, a beautiful dark-eyed man had also greeted the day with a beaming smile. She was sure of it.

Val Santisi didn't know what he was missing. She would have seduced him, cheerfully, deliberately, and with great creativity. This love she felt, although greatly spiritual, seemed to demand an amazing amount of physical expression. She wanted to give and give and give to him; *My body is yours, I trust you, I love you, do what you will.*

Life was so very fine.

She stretched and wiggled her feet, then realized one of her socks had come off during the night. Bare toes were hunting through the sheets when they encountered something small and square, with the slick texture of plastic or vinyl. Definitely not a warm, woolly sock. Frowning, she shrugged off Val's jacket so she would have hands, then tossed the sheets off the bed. There it was at the bottom of the mattress, a brown vinyl case with a snap front that looked as if it could have been used to hold eyeglasses. Except the case was obviously filled with something more symmetrical than eyeglasses.

Her first thought was that it must have fallen from one of the pockets of Val's jacket. But, no . . . she recalled distinctively both pockets had been empty the night before. For some reason she felt strangely apprehensive about touching the case, as if it might suddenly turn into a snake and bite her.

But she was a reporter and a woman and very curious, a combination that was impossible to fight.

She picked up the case and pulled open the snap, shaking a half-dozen cards out on the bed. Some were laminated in plastic or encased in leather folders, others were common, run-of-the-mill business cards. All were identifications of some sort or another, and several included a photograph. In every case the photograph was of Val Santisi.

It didn't make sense. It was unthinkable. Still . . .

The business addresses on the cards varied from Washington to New York to Palm Beach. A variety of names and professions were represented—an exterminator, a security analyst, a plumber, a census taker, an aluminum-siding salesman . . . and yes, a policeman. The badge he had shown her on Christmas Eve was right there on the bed along with everything else. Just as authentic-looking. And just as phony?

She was shaking, but she didn't feel cold. She didn't feel anything. She picked up the black leather jacket with numb fingers, turning it inside out. There, sewn into the lining near the hem with awkward, uneven stitches, was a tiny zipper, halfopen. A homemade pocket, just the thing for hiding those pesky identifications you don't happen to be using at the time.

Fumbling a bit, she replaced everything in the vinyl case, then put the case in her purse on the bedside table. Feeling as if she were sleepwalking, she took an ice-cold shower, barely aware of the stinging pinpricks of water on her skin. Any logical thought was hopelessly mired in memories and questions and fears. He'd lied about his profession. What else had he lied about?

No. No, he wouldn't lie to me. There has to be an explanation. Something to do with undercover work for the police department . . . ?

It was a long shot, but she had to know. She dressed, then called Dylan at the office.

"You're alive!" Dylan's cheerful voice seemed to attack her through the receiver. "I was afraid those sneaky Indians had got the best of you."

"I'm fine," Nicki said woodenly. "Dylan, I want you to do me a favor. Do you still have your source inside the police department?"

"If by 'source' you mean my cousin Lauralee, then the answer is yes. She works in Dispatch."

"I need to know if Val Santisi works as a detective for the Ninth Precinct. Can you find out?"

Silence. Then: "Can't *you?* I thought you two grew up together. I got the impression you knew each other pretty well."

"I thought we did too." Nicki couldn't keep her voice from shaking. "I'm going to work at home this morning, so call me back here as soon as you find out. Thanks, Dylan."

She hung up the receiver, then went straight to the secret stash in her closet and pulled out a half-dozen pieces of gum. Chewing ferociously, she sat down at her computer and stared at the dark screen for five minutes before she remembered to turn on the power. She needn't have bothered. She could think of nothing to write, nothing to say. She had never felt more helpless in her life.

Dylan came by the apartment at noon. The somber expression he wore was new to her. Hands pushed deep in the pockets of his overcoat, shoulders hunched, he positioned his narrow, worried face two inches in front of Nicki's nose.

"Did Val Santisi tell you he was a cop?" he demanded shortly.

"Is he?" Nicki's lips felt stiff, fighting the words.

"He is not now, nor has he ever been, an employee of the Washington Police Department. If he told you he was, he was lying. Simple as that."

Nicki sat down on the edge of the sofa. After a moment Dylan sat down next to her.

"Dammit," he muttered. "I knew you weren't going to like this."

"No," she whispered.

"Would you like to talk about it?"

"I can't. Not yet."

"Nicki . . . just how involved are you with this guy?"

She felt her face flame. "Involved."

Dylan winced. "I was afraid of that. Look, if there's anything I can do to help you—"

"No." She hadn't meant the word to come out so abruptly. She took a deep breath and closed her eyes, rubbing her temples with her fingers. "I'm sorry, Dylan. I appreciate the information. I just need some time to think now."

"Okay. I understand." Dylan gave her an awkward, brotherly hug, then stood up. "Look, I realize this is none of my business, but . . . if I were you, I'd steer clear of this guy. I've seen the type before. They like to impress women, and they don't mind lying to do it. You may have grown up with Val Santisi, but apparently you don't know him very well."

"Apparently not." Nicki followed him to the door, vaguely surprised that her legs held her. She wasn't feeling very steady. "Thanks for the information, Dylan."

"And for making your day so cheery and bright?" Dylan replied morosely. "Little Mary Sunshine, that's me. I swear, I don't know what the world is coming to these days. Seems like everyone you meet is either a liar, a thief, or a victim. Could you believe what happened to poor Calvin Fleming this weekend?"

Calvin Fleming was the owner of the *Observer*, a feisty, self-made millionaire with a reputation for enjoying the ladies, despite his seventy-odd years. "What are you talking about?" Nicki asked. "Something happened to Mr. Fleming?"

"You didn't hear the news? Where have you been all weekend?" Mercifully Dylan didn't give Nicki an opportunity to answer. "Fleming hosted a thousand-dollar-a-plate dinner Friday night for Congressman What's-his-bucket . . . remember, we were talking about it at the Zephyr Club? Anyway, somewhere between the shrimp cocktails and the cheesecake and all the speeches, Jimmy Valentine managed to clean out the floor safe in the master bedroom and the wall safe in the library, *plus* walk off with a custom-made gold-plated chess set worth a fortune. And this all happened with seventy-five guests in the house, not to mention the hired help. No one can figure out how he got out of there without being seen. The chess pieces alone must have weighed fifty pounds. Hell's bells, he'd need a shopping cart to carry everything out. The man is not human."

Friday night.

The same night she had pleaded with Val to stay with her . . . and he'd refused. He'd been half-frozen when he'd returned to her apartment Saturday morning. What was it he had said to her? *I think I went a little farther than I should have tonight.*

Nicki opened the door with ice-cold fingers. Her mind was spinning, whipping everything into place with nauseating precision. It all fit. It was impossible, it was unbelievable, it was preposterous . . . but it all fit.

"Take care," Dylan way saying. "Doors and windows locked, all that sort of stuff. You never know where this Jimmy Valentine is going to turn up next."

"You're right. You never know."

Dylan paused in the doorway, shuffling his feet. "About Santisi . . . I'm sorry, Nicki. If you need anyone to talk to, I'm a pretty good listener."

She tried to smile, but it was a painful process. "I'm just fine, Dylan."

"Yeah, sure," he said glumly. "And I'm Jimmy Valentine."

Eight

Nicki dressed to kill. It fit her mood.

She wore a white satin *bustier* that revealed more than it covered, and a narrow black velvet miniskirt. Her black stockings were shot through with silver glitter, and the diamond studs in her ears matched the hard gleam in her eyes. Her hair was deliberately disheveled in a wild black mane, and a dozen silver bracelets jangled on her arm.

She was prepared. She was a big girl. She could take care of herself . . . and she was damn well going to take care of Val Santisi as well.

He arrived at her apartment at five to eight. His golden-brown hair was still damp, he'd nicked his chin shaving, and his tie wasn't quite straight. He looked . . . *edgy* was the only word Nicki could come up with.

"You're beautiful," he said, instead of hello. There

was a grim note in his voice that didn't quite match the compliment.

"You couldn't tell it by the look on your face," Nicki replied. "Is something wrong? Don't you like the way I'm dressed?"

"I like the way you're dressed."

"Oh," she said. "Then it must be something else. Are you angry with me?"

He rolled his eyes. "No. Why would I be angry with you?"

"Why, indeed?" Nicki murmured, going to the closet for her coat. "You're not acting like yourself, Val. Did you have a bad day?"

"Yes."

"That's a shame. Did the bad guys get away?"

He looked blank. "Bad guys?"

"You're a policeman, darling," Nicki reminded him, wide-eyed and innocent. "Isn't that what you do, chase after bad guys?"

A shadow fell over his face. "If we don't hurry, we'll miss our reservations. Are you ready to go?"

For a moment Nicki's heart was lodged in her burning throat, blocking her words. If she had had any doubts about Val lying to her, any fragile hope that it all might have been some ridiculous misunderstanding, the look on his face was enough to convince her otherwise. He wasn't a policeman.

Which raised the interesting question: What exactly *was* he?

"Oh, I'm ready," she said, lifting her chin and willing away the tears that stung her eyes. "In fact, I can hardly wait."

The drive to the restaurant was relatively silent.

Val had brought the rental car again. Nicki stared at the "U-Drive-Us" sticker on the windshield, wondering if Val Santisi even owned a car. He'd said it was in the shop being repaired, but what did that signify? She didn't know what to believe anymore. The night was cold and cheerless, the city was lost in fog, and her heart was breaking. Those were the only certainties in her life at the moment.

He took her to Antoine's, possibly the best French restaurant in Washington. He must have bribed the maître d' well, for they were seated at a lovely table near a window. Their waiter described the specials of the day with elaborate hand gestures and heartfelt enthusiasm. When neither Val nor Nicki exhibited the proper interest, he sniffed and informed them he would return in a few moments when they had had time to consider.

"Now we've done it," Val said, trying for a smile. "He's ticked off. The service will probably be lousy."

"You shouldn't have brought me here." Nicki kept her gaze lowered, sketching teardrops on the tablecloth with her fingernail. She didn't want to look at Val, didn't want to look into those beautiful dark eyes that had kept so many secrets so well. It hurt too much. "It can't be easy to afford a meal like this on a policeman's salary. It makes me feel terribly guilty."

His silence told her she had again hit a nerve. She took a sip of water, smiling grimly. *Baby, you ain't seen nothin' yet.*

She continued biding her time throughout dinner. She chatted and gazed idly around the room, pretending not to notice Val's silence. She ate, ignoring the fact he hardly touched his food. It wasn't until dessert was served—*crème brulée* with chocolate-dipped strawberries—that she looked him straight in the eye, taking what felt like her first breath of the evening.

"Could I ask you a question?" she asked politely.

Val gave her a faint smile. "Let me guess. You want to know why I've been so quiet tonight."

"Oh, no," she replied, waving her hand. "I couldn't care less about that. You see, I already know you're a liar. What I want to know now is if you're a thief as well. Do you steal things for a living?"

She had expected quite a reaction, and he didn't disappoint her. He dropped his spoon. His body grew visibly taut. His eyes narrowed to slits.

"What did you say?" His voice was low and hoarse.

"*Do . . . you . . . steal . . . things?*" Nicki repeated, enunciating each word with venomous precision. "What part of the question don't you understand?"

"Do I steal things?" He gave a shaky, disbelieving laugh. "Is this some kind of joke?"

"Oh, it's no joke. And you're not answering my question."

"I don't understand why the hell you would *ask* the question. What happened in the past twenty-four hours that made you decide I was a thief?"

"And a liar," she snapped. "Don't forget that part."

He spoke slowly, as if the words were painful. "No, I won't forget. Talk to me."

"Words are so imprecise." She reached beneath the table for her purse. She pulled out the brown vinyl case she had found in her bed that morning d tossed it on the table. "I believe this says it all. I ink it fell out of that little pocket in the lining of ur leather jacket."

He stared at the case, the muscle in his cheek rking and pulling, uncontrolled. "I'm so sorry." He oke through his teeth. "I never meant for you to d out this way."

"That's the funny part." Her lips curled in a bitter nile. "I don't know *what* I found out! Are you a umber? Are you a salesman? A census taker? The t is endless. About the only thing I do know is that u're *not* a policeman. Dylan checked with a friend his in the police department. They've never heard you."

"Dylan. Good old Dylan." Val's voice was bleak. Iow interesting."

"You lied to me."

He dropped his head against the back of the chair, adowed eyes fixed on her white face. "Yes. I lied to u."

Just like that. Anger and betrayal formed a wind-orm in Nicki's mind. "You're a bastard."

"I imagine I am," he said flatly. "But the one thing n not is a thief. Despite what you think—"

"You lied about the reason you were in my apart-ent on Christmas Eve."

He swallowed hard. *I deserve this,* he thought. es."

"And you were lying when you told me you were red as security for the Knights' party."

"Yes."

"Tell me one more thing." Her voice shook. Her

whole body trembled. "When you left me Frida
night, where did you go?"

"I was going to tell you tonight. I was going
explain—"

She crumpled up her genuine linen napkin an
threw it in his dark face. "Friday night," she groun
out softly, dangerously close to tears. "You didr
happen to pay a little visit to Calvin Fleming's hom
did you?"

"All right. *Yes.* I went to Fleming's house. But yo
have to understand—"

"Oh, I'm beginning to understand very well. Yo
say you love me, then you lie to me over and over
Nicki closed her eyes. She felt as if she were frozen
ice. She couldn't move, she couldn't think. Her hea
was bowed; pain and confusion pressed in on h
from all sides, making her smaller, tighter, takir
her breath away. "You haven't changed all th
much from the old days on Newton Street, have yo
You're still looking out for number one, whatever
costs. I should have known. I can't believe I was su
a fool."

"I never lied to you about the way I feel." V
reached over the table and caught her hand, pres
ing it hard. "That's the important thing. The re
of it . . . if you'll just give me a chance, I ca
explain—"

"I'm sure you can." She shook him off, her blu
eyes hard. "You're so *good* at explanations. Yo
should have been the writer, you know that? Yo
have a wonderful imagination. Come to think of
you could very well be a writer. Or a con artist, or

t burglar . . . you could be anything. How should know? I'm just the woman you slept with."

The expression on his face was like the deathly alm in the center of a hurricane. "Don't ever talk ke that. Don't even think like that. You know what u are to me." *Everything. Everything . . .*

"I don't know anything." Her voice rang out loud ough for all the room to hear. "And I'm not sure I ant to know. Maybe the truth is worse than the lies. don't know." She sent a wild, bright-eyed look ound the room. "Everyone's staring. I have to get ut of here. Don't you try to stop me. Don't you dare y to stop me."

Then she was up and across the room, walking at rst, then running, zigzagging around tables and odging startled waiters. Val felt helpless and sick as e watched her dash out the front door. She'd rgotten her coat, he thought, his heart feeling like bleeding wound in his chest. She was such a little ing . . . she would freeze, dressed like that. She eeded her coat.

What have I done to you?

And finally he faced a painful truth. In the past he ad always believed the end justified the means . . . nd he'd been wrong.

Her heart was broken.

Nicki was sure of it, her heart was literally broken a million crazy pieces. There was a tangible physical ain deep, deep within her. She sat hunched in e backseat of a taxi, arms wrapped around her are shoulders, shivering outside, shivering inside.

She felt as if she had nothing and no one in the worl to depend on but herself. Which was nothing new.

Who was Val Santisi? What was he? She didn even know.

"We're running the meter pretty high, lady," th cabdriver said. "You sure you want to keep drivin around like this? You got anywhere in particular yo want to go?"

It had been nearly an hour since she'd left th restaurant. She hadn't wanted to go straight hom in case he followed her. By now she was probabl safe. She gave the driver the address of her apar ment building, then asked if he couldn't turn th heater up.

"Most folks wear a coat on a night like this," h replied sourly. "You should take better care of you self, lady."

She had been home just long enough to chang into her ugly green robe and smear cold cream a over her face when Val began pounding on her doo

"Come on, Squeaky. Open up."

She thought about calling Security and havin him tossed out of the building. That was tempting

"I'm not going away," he shouted at the top of hi voice. "Not until you've listened to me."

She thought about pretending she wasn't home.

"I know you're in there, Squeaky. I can see th light under the door."

"Leave me alone, and *don't call me Squeaky*!" Sh kicked the door with her bare foot, then clapped he hand over her mouth and hopped around on one foo until the pain subsided. "That door is going to stay locked," she gasped out when she could talk again. "And you can just go to hell!"

"I did. I am. Open the door."

"Bugger off."

"Suit yourself." There was a short silence, then a faint scratching at the lock. The door swung wide, and Val walked in, closing it neatly behind him with a nudge of his shoe. "You should get an alarm system," he said tonelessly. "That lock is obsolete. A five-year-old could pick it."

Nicki gaped at him as he went straight to the wounded hero's recliner and sat down. "What do you think you're doing?"

Val stared into the dark, cold fireplace, his face set in stone. "I'm waiting."

"For what?"

"I thought you might want to wash that stuff off your face before we talk. Women are usually sensitive about things like that. I don't want you to feel uncomfortable. I want your complete attention."

She remembered the cold cream and flushed darkly. Fortunately he couldn't tell what color she was beneath her rose-scented marinade. "I'm just fine the way I am. If you don't like it, you're welcome to leave. As a matter of fact, I wish you would leave."

"I'm sure you do. But I'll go when I've said what I came to say."

"Buggers," she muttered, and stalked off to the bathroom.

Five minutes later she was back, still in her ugly green robe but with a freshly scrubbed face and her hair tugged back in a ruthless-looking bun. Val was down on his haunches in front of the fireplace, setting a match to a freshly laid fire.

"I thought we could use a little warmth," he said, leaning forward to blow on the flickering flame. "There's a definite chill in this room."

"Don't get too comfortable." She stood behind him, her arms folded across her chest. "You have two minutes, then I'm calling the police. The *real* police," she added scornfully. "There's a reward for information leading to Jimmy Valentine's arrest, you know. I could turn you in and buy a savings bond for my retirement."

"Now there's an interesting point." Val rose to his feet, brushing his hands off on his pants. "Why *haven't* you called the police? You're a respectable, law-abiding citizen. You have a duty to tell them what you know and save the world, don't you think?"

"Oh, this is rich." Nicki's smile was shaky, something close to tears. "You came over here to talk me into turning you in?"

"No. I never worried about your calling the police. You couldn't."

"Then you're a very foolish man," she said stonily. "And you're wrong."

"No . . . I'm right." There was a bleak conviction in his voice. "You know me better than anyone else in the world. You know my fears and my failings . . . and my limits. In your heart you could never convince yourself I was a thief, no matter how damning the evidence."

"What do you mean, I *know you?* How on earth can you say that? I'll tell you what I know about you, Val: I know you keep secrets, and I know you tell lies.

I know you're charming and convincing and a pro at picking locks. I know you liked to break the rules when you were growing up, and you like to break the rules now. That about sums up what I know about you."

"Now who's lying?" He closed his hands into fists, wanting to pull her close, knowing he couldn't. "We've shared everything two people can share. You know I love you. You know I'd never hurt you."

She smiled a little, bitterly. "Don't kid yourself. You already did."

All the breath seemed to go out of him. He closed his eyes briefly, feeling his muscles knot with panic. She was right.

He said hoarsely, "I didn't expect to love you."

"Then you don't mind lying to people you *don't* love?"

"Yes. No. Hell, I don't even know what I'm saying." He rubbed his hand over the back of his neck, sending her a dark, frustrated look through his lashes. "This isn't going anywhere. Will you please sit down and just . . . listen to me? Will you give me that much?"

She wanted to point out just how much she'd given him already but clamped down on the words with a mighty effort. She went to the sofa and sat down, hiding her trembling hands in her lap and looking at him expressionlessly. The sooner he had his say, the sooner he would leave, and the sooner she could fall apart.

Val held her empty gaze as long as he could, then stared past her, at his own mirrored reflection in the window. "I don't live in Washington. I'm here on business. I'm a private investigator for AIA—American International Assurance—in New York. For the past year—"

"American International Assurance?" Nicki echoed in a tight voice. "I haven't heard that name before. Do you have business cards for that one too?"

His lips tightened. "I'm telling you the truth. I travel all over the world. It's my job to recover stolen merchandise and expose insurance frauds. You know what they say." He smiled without humor. "It takes one to know one. I came to a point in my life about eight years ago when I realized I could either find a legitimate job that took advantage of my . . . dubious talents . . . or I could become another Good-time Grady, a con artist always looking for a new mark. I wanted . . . something real, something I could build on. I've been with AIA for nearly three years. I was with a smaller insurance company for a couple of years before that. I'm good at what I do. I don't always follow the rules—old habits are hard to break—but I usually get results."

Nicki's eyes were intense as they watched him, huge and accusing in her pale face. "If all this is true—and I'm not saying I believe you—why couldn't you just tell me in the beginning? Why all the lies?"

"This is the hard part," Val muttered. He lifted both his hands, pressing hard against his eyes. "About nine months ago I was sent down to Palm Beach to investigate the theft of an emerald necklace insured by AIA. It was just one in a long string of robberies; no one had a clue who was responsible. The thief seemed to know everything: guest lists of parties, which homes would be vacant and for how long, the location of hidden safes . . . I swear, every time a Palm Beach socialite received a valuable gift from her husband, he found out about it. He had his finger on everything."

"Just like . . ." Nicki's voice trailed off. She looked up at him. "Just like Jimmy Valentine?"

"One and the same. When I was in Palm Beach, I posed as a magazine writer researching an article on America's most prominent families. I started going to all the right parties, listening to the gossip, learning who was going where with whom. I knew who was wearing paste, who wore the real thing and how much it cost. I could have planned ten robberies myself with the idle chitchat I heard. That's when I realized my thief was no common garden-variety crook. All the inside information I gathered, he obviously had access to as well. Either he moved in high society himself, or he stayed very close to the people who did. I knew if I wanted to catch him, I'd have to start thinking like a professional criminal."

"That couldn't have been too hard," Nicki muttered, in a tone she knew would aggravate him. "Great minds think alike."

"I tried to anticipate him," he replied in a grating voice, shoving his hands into the pockets of his overcoat. "I tried to figure out what I would do in his place, assuming he had access to the same inside information I did. After a couple of humbling miscalculations, I hit pay dirt. I was staking out a big house on the beach one night when I saw him."

Try as she might, Nicki couldn't maintain her air of cynical indifference. "You actually saw his face? You could identify him?"

"Not exactly." Val felt himself flushing. "It was pitch-black, and he happened to be on the roof at the time. I watched him rappel down to a window on the second story, then I went to my car and called the police. They arrived within five minutes, but they didn't find a thing. He'd just . . . vanished. After that, the robberies stopped. I went back to New York and kept my eyes on the police reports. A few months later Jimmy Valentine surfaced again in Washington. I flew down here a couple of weeks before Christmas and rented a car and an apartment. Whatever it took to nail this guy, I was willing to do it."

Nicki ducked her head, her hands clenched in her lap. "Obviously."

His lips tightened. "I started reading Nicki Sharman's column in the *Observer*. I needed information on the movers and shakers, and I thought a gossip columnist was just the person to provide it. I had no idea Nicki Sharman and Squeaky Boggs were one and the same." His gaze rested on her for a quiet moment. "When you found me here on Christmas Eve, I'd just finished copying all the engagements in your Daytimer for the next few weeks. I'd also been through your desk and read the notes for your next column, and I'd made a list of names, addresses, and phone numbers from your Rolodex."

"I see." Her throat was painfully tight; every word hurt. "It must have been a shock when you realized who I was. What a good thing you were carrying your handy-dandy detective badge, and with your real name on it too. I suppose you keep it for those sticky moments when you run into someone from your past. You think of everything, don't you?"

Val felt himself growing colder. "I was doing my job the way I've always done. Someone hands me a puzzle that can't be solved, and I solve it any way I can. It's a challenge, a game I play for the fun and the hell of it. That's all."

"That's all?" Nicki stood up, a high flush burning on her cheeks. She wanted to hit him and probably would have had he been within swinging range. "What do you mean, that's all? You *use* me, you lie to me, you break my heart, and then you call it a game? I have news for you, *Detective*. If you want to play your game, go ahead, but don't you dare play it with me."

"It's not like that," Val said hoarsely. This was the hardest thing he had ever done, watching something so bright and beautiful slip away from him, knowing he had no one to blame but himself. "The way I feel about you has nothing to do with my job. It's separate, it's . . . real."

"That must be hard for you, trying to decide what's real and what isn't."

"No," he whispered, with a faint shake of his head. "When you've waited all your life for something, you recognize it right away. You know how precious it is, because you know how rare it is."

"That's what I always thought." Her voice was brittle, her eyes stinging with tears. Her heart felt so heavy in her chest, made of cold lead. *I won't cry, I won't.* "Now I don't know what to believe. I'm confused. I'm angry. Love isn't supposed to be this way. It's not supposed to hurt you and disappoint you and leave you feeling alone and frustrated. It's not something you do just for the fun and the hell of it."

"I never thought it was." He knew he should have told her everything in the beginning; he'd botched the whole thing, and he couldn't blame her for being angry. More than anything in the world, he wanted her respect and her trust, but when he looked into her accusing blue eyes, he was a hopeless fraud. "If I could go back, if I could do things differently, I would. But I can't. The only thing I can do is ask you to believe me when I say I never meant to hurt you."

"Is that supposed to make me feel better?"

"No." Hopelessness seemed to be seeping deep inside him. He wanted to reach for her, to hold her in his arms and make her feel safe and cherished and cared for. He wanted to be something wonderful in her eyes, but he knew it was too late for that. "What's done is done. For a while there I think I actually believed it all myself. I believed I'd find an easy way out of all this, but I was dreaming. I'm not the man you want me to be." He smiled, and it wasn't a pleasant smile. "Hell, I'm not even the man I want to be."

There was a silence that seemed to go on forever. Nicki stared down at her fretting, ice-cold fingers and said hoarsely, "That's your excuse for this whole charade? You're just not the man you want to be?"

His dark eyes focused on her bent head with a brooding intensity. "It's not a charade. Our relationship—"

She looked up at him with the ice of attack. "What relationship? You can't have a relationship based on lies. You don't have the faintest idea how to have a relationship. You just keep sliding by on good looks and smooth talk, taking the easy way out every chance you get."

His knees felt unsteady; he wished he had something to lean against. He felt vulnerable and pathetic, as if he were a kid again and his old man's fist was heading for his face. "Funny you see it like that." His voice was slightly hoarse. "I don't feel like I had it easy. You never knew my folks real well, did you? They were a sterling example of love at home, I'll tell you. Completely devoted to each other and to the bottle—not necessarily in that order."

"And my mother died when I was born, and my father could never quite bring himself to forgive me. That's just the way things were—we both started out with some disadvantages. But I never used that as an excuse for not becoming the person I knew I wanted to be."

His eyes narrowed. "Believe me, your life was a picnic compared to—"

"So who said life was going to be fair?" Her emotions scratched and tore at her voice. "There comes a time when you either turn your back on the past or you let it cripple you forever. I haven't settled for second rate in a long, long time, and I'll be damned if I'm going to start now. I'm *special*! If you want to do a number on someone, you're looking at the wrong lady. I deserve better!"

"I know that." He turned away abruptly. "You deserve the best."

She watched him walk to the door, anger and frustration pressing against her chest, making it painful to breathe. He was leaving. He wasn't going to stay and fight for her, to try to work this through. True to form, Val Santisi was taking the easy way out rather than risk putting himself on the line. "I thought I had the best," she said, her voice low and scornful. "Obviously I was wrong. You're so afraid of finding out what you're really made of, you won't even *try* and hold on to me."

He stopped halfway across the room, keeping his back to her, his shoulders square and rigid. "I'm doing the right thing. You may not think so now—"

"No!" Nicki shook her head fiercely. "You're doing the easiest thing, just like you did when you lied to me. That was easier than to risk telling me the truth and losing me. And now losing me is easier than trying to keep me and failing."

"What do you know about what I feel?" He whirled on her, dark eyes blazing in his pale face. "Do you honestly think this is *easy* for me? Facing reality isn't exactly a joyride, sweetheart, but facts are facts. I have nothing to offer you."

"I never asked for anything," Nicki shot back, "except yourself."

He stared at her, absolutely confounded. "You're trying to tell me you still want me, after everything that's happened?"

Nicki tossed back her head and gave him a flying finger. "Right now I wouldn't have you if you came gift-wrapped on a silver platter! You're still living back on Newton Street, hedging your bets, watching your back, keeping an ace up your sleeve. I won't settle for half of anything, and that's all you're willing to give. I want it all—love, trust, loyalty, commitment—the whole nine yards. I want someone who will give me the very best of himself, because that's what I intend to give him!"

"You want a damned fairy tale!"

"That's right! And you know what? I'm going to *have* my damned fairy tale, with you or without you!" She marched past him, opening the front door and throwing it wide. "Here you go, Santisi. The easiest way out."

The fire in her eyes and the force of her convictions staggered him. She wasn't bluffing. Feisty Squeaky Boggs, with a china doll's face and a spine of tempered steel. He'd thought he'd understood her strength and spirit, but he hadn't even come close.

For a moment the fierce swell of admiration he experienced for such an incredible woman overwhelmed every other emotion. He drank her in with his eyes and his heart and his soul, the proud angle of her head and shoulders, the riot of color in her cheeks, the funny way her robe dragged on the floor. She would be fine without him, she truly would. She was a survivor. She was a champion.

Slowly, unsteadily, he walked past her. In the hallway he turned, swallowing hard over the desperate block in his throat. "The best of me." His voice was soft, slightly hoarse. "What is that, I wonder? What could I possibly give you?"

"All or nothing." Nicki was amazed at her outward control, when inside it felt as if she were breaking apart. "I mean that. Start believing in yourself, believing in *us* . . . or don't ever come near me again."

He opened his mouth as if he needed to say something more. Whatever he saw in her face must have changed his mind, because he jammed his hands in the pockets of his coat and left without another word.

Nicki closed the door quietly and carefully, then took a sobbing breath and yanked it open again, slamming it shut with enough force to rattle the pictures on the walls. How could she have been such a fool? Val Santisi loved her—she knew it with every fiber of her being—but he wasn't going to fight for her. There was an instant of pure, unadulterated panic as she contemplated the prospect of never laughing with him again, never holding him, never trusting in him again.

Was that what she wanted? Worse yet, was that what *he* wanted?

She made herself a cup of tea, then poured it down the sink when her heaving stomach protested. She looked at the clock. It was midnight. Time to go to sleep. If she concentrated on the simple routines of a normal existence, hopefully she could keep her emotions at bay.

But when the phone rang an hour later, she was lying in bed with her swollen, red-rimmed eyes glued to the ceiling.

"Nicki?"

It was Val. She couldn't think when he'd last called her Nicki. Oddly the sound of her given name made her feel more alone and lost than she did already. "Yes?"

"I forgot to tell you something."

Unaccountably her heart leapt. "What?"

"I want you to be careful. This business with

Jimmy Valentine . . . you could be more deeply involved in it than you realize."

Her heart fell. "What do you mean?"

"Dylan."

Disappointment—though she didn't know what she had been hoping for—made her voice tight. "What *about* Dylan?"

"How long has he worked at the paper?"

"I don't know . . . six months, maybe more."

"What did he do before that?"

"I think he said something about backpacking through Europe last summer. Why would you—" She stopped abruptly, sitting up in bed. "Are you trying to tell me you suspect Dylan of being Jimmy Valentine? *Dylan?*"

"I'm trying to tell you to be very, very careful. When we were at the Zephyr Club on Friday, I noticed how interested Dylan was in your work, in all the gossip that comes your way. I've never seen anyone ask so many questions."

"That's just Dylan."

"What about Serena Grace? Obviously he manages to keep her happy, and happiness for a woman like Serena Grace does not come cheap. I doubt his reporter's salary stretches to cover exotic dancers."

"I'm not going to listen to you accuse Dylan of—"

"I don't have enough evidence yet to accuse anyone of anything. But there's one more thing I want you to think about. After I left you on Friday night, I told you I went to Calvin Fleming's house. Do you know why? Because at dinner Dylan had been so incredibly interested in hearing all about the party the guy was throwing. If he had something up his

sleeve, I wanted to be there." He paused. "And h
did, obviously. I just wish I knew how the hell h
pulled it off without my seeing anything."

"This is crazy. I would know if Dylan was hidin
something from me."

"Not necessarily." Val's voice was curiously de
tached. "I managed to get away with it. Who's to sa
Dylan's any different?"

"*Touché.*" Biting her lip, she carefully replaced th
receiver. She was cold. She pulled the covers aroun
her, up to her pink, sniffling nose, around her ears

Hiding. Whether from herself or from the world
she didn't know.

Nine

Bonjour, esteemed colleague! I come bearing *très bien* munchies for your coffee break. May I come in?"

Caught off guard, Nicki swallowed her gum. Eyes watering, gasping softly for air, she managed to nod.

Oblivious, Dylan strode into her office, bowing and placing a jelly-filled doughnut on her desk with a flourish. "You've been much too quiet this morning," he said. "I thought you could do with a nice sugar rush."

"Merci," Nicki managed hoarsely, deliberately keeping her gaze lowered. She wasn't sure what Dylan would see in her eyes, thanks to the seed of doubt Val had planted. "I didn't eat breakfast this morning. I guess it's showing."

"Oui, oui," Dylan replied breezily. He took a giant-size bite of his own doughnut, chomping enthusiastically. "You're very lucky to have me here. I'm not

only good-looking and boyishly charming, I'm in
credibly thoughtful."

"Not to mention bilingual." Nicki's smile felt rigid
against her cheeks. "Did you learn French when you
were in Europe last summer?"

Dylan grinned. "Do I sound as if I know what I'm
doing? I don't. You've just heard the full extent of my
French vocabulary. I did learn a few down-to-earth
phrases in Italian, but I won't repeat them."

"Thank you." Nicki had never had any trouble
talking to Dylan before, but today it was all she could
manage to carry on a polite conversation. Her con
fusion was too fresh, too overwhelming. Could this
incredibly average-looking fellow with wire-rimmed
glasses and stooped shoulders possibly be the sin
ister Jimmy Valentine? She tried to envision Dylan
Lichter with a stocking mask pulled over his face.

It was hard.

"What the heck are you looking at?" Dylan de
manded, rearing back his head. "Your eyes are all
squinty. Do I have frosting on my face?"

"Uh . . . a little on your chin." Flushing, Nicki
looked down at the doodle marks on her desk blot
ter. Question marks, little hearts cracked down the
middle with a jagged line, more question marks. How
Freudian. "Don't mind me, Dylan . . . I'm just pre
occupied. You know how I get when I'm working on
something."

"Judging by the look on your face, you must be
privy to some heavy gossip. What's up? I'll bet it's
political. We haven't had a juicy political scandal for
a while. Did one of our elected officials do something
naughty this weekend? Oh, I know. Old Senator

Whoozit—the bald guy with all the chins—took his secretary to Atlantic City again and won the million-dollar jackpot. That rascal has more energy than I do."

"You ought to be writing for the scandal sheets," Nicki said, toying with the pen in her hand. She couldn't help but remember all the times Dylan had questioned her about her work, her plans, the inside scoop on the movers and shakers. She'd assumed he was merely curious.

Of course he was merely curious. He was a curious type, that's all. This whole thing was laughable. If it hadn't been for Val putting doubts in her head, she would never have suspected Dylan in a million years.

"I do have a flair for drama," Dylan admitted modestly. "When I retire, I believe I'll try my hand at writing a book. A thriller, a steamy page-turner with scx and murder and mayhem and all the exciting stuff. There's nothing like a good mystery to challenge the mind, don't you think?"

Nicki stared at him. Was she paranoid, or did everything Dylan say suddenly have a double meaning? "I suppose not. I didn't know you enjoyed mysteries."

"You forget how often I'm assigned to the food pages. When you spend long, boring days typing up chowder and casserole recipes, you need all the excitement you can get."

Nicki became aware that an idea was taking shape in her mind. A plan, and not a bad one for a woman who was utterly bereft, without dreams, without joy.

One way or another, she had to know whether Val was right about Dylan.

She forced a smile, hoping Dylan couldn't hear the nerves in her voice. "Believe it or not, when you make your living writing about the lifestyles of the rich and richer, things can get just as monotonous. Shall I tell you the most exciting tidbit I've come across this week? Ambassador Devonshire and his wife are sneaking off to Los Angeles next weekend for secret his and hers face-lifts and tummy tucks."

Dylan chuckled. "Isn't that romantic? I believe I'll alert the media. We should have someone at the airport to take before-and-after pictures."

"No, the Devonshires can keep their little secret. I refuse to stoop so low as to publicize their nips and tucks. My word, how would it be to have nothing more serious to worry about than whether or not your tummy was flat?"

"When you have as much money as they do, it's probably a real challenge to find things to worry about."

"I wouldn't mind that kind of challenge," Nicki replied wistfully. "Do you know what the good ambassador gave his lovely wife for Christmas? A Fabergé egg, the most exquisite thing I have ever seen in my life. It must have cost an absolute fortune, even by the Devonshires' standards."

"I heard she was an airline stewardess before she married him." Dylan shook his shaggy blond head. "Life is so unfair. Oh, well, now that we're both good and depressed, I'll let you get back to work. Enjoy your doughnut. It's not a jeweled egg, but it's the thought that counts." He closed the door, then opened it again almost immediately. "One more thing—your buddy, Val Santisi . . . how did all that work out? Did you find out what the fellow was up to?"

Startled, Nicki dropped her pen on the carpet. She picked it up, taking those few seconds to compose her expression. "You were right," she said. "He actually works for a pest-control company. He thought I'd be more impressed if I were going out with Dirty Harry. Needless to say, he wasn't looking for a lasting relationship."

"That's a definite bummer." Dylan scowled at his wing tips, then lifted his head and gave Nicki a rueful smile. "I guess this is one of the moments in life when some obnoxious person tells you to count your blessings. 'Tis a far, far better man you deserve than Val Santisi."

"Thank you, Dylan." Nicki kept her smile on her face until he'd closed the door, then groaned and dropped her forehead in her hands. She felt incredibly guilty. She could not believe it to be true, that Dylan Lichter could be a gawky, endearing reporter by day and a wily cat burglar by night. Still, the unresolved possibility would haunt her until she proved to herself—and to Val—otherwise. Her impulsive little trap was set. Now all she could do was pray that no one took the bait.

Nicki never took her eyes off him.

He walked slowly across the snow-dusted ground toward her, moving with the cautious, measured step of a man who wasn't entirely sure of his welcome. A bright, cold breeze tumbled his hair in all directions, spinning gold with brown. Despite the clear, cold afternoon, his leather jacket hung open, showing the broad gray and navy stripes of a thick wool sweater. His jeans were ancient, more white than blue, and his sneakers were tied with fluorescent yellow laces.

He might have been a teenager again. He still radiated that "ready for anything" attitude, thumbs hooked in the pockets of his jeans, lips pressed tight. Only as he came closer could Nicki see the shadows of a sleepless night beneath his eyes. A pair of dark glasses hid her own shadows.

"Thanks for meeting me here," she said, although she had to clear her throat twice before the words came out.

Val sent a curious glance around the deserted park, then looked down at Nicki. She was sitting on a swing crusted with yesterday's snow, her gloved fingers curling around the rusty chains on either side. Her hair was pulled loosely to one side with a black ribbon, and the tips of her ears were bright red. He could barely see her tiny nose beneath a pair of oversize sunglasses.

He couldn't tell her how much he'd missed her in just fourteen hours, how pretty she looked, how she should have worn a hat to keep warm. It was too late for that.

"My curiosity has been eating me alive since you called," he said. "What's up?"

"This is business," Nicki said.

Val's lips tightened. "Of course."

They were both so cool, Nicki thought. So . . .

careful. Was it possible they had shared so much love and laughter only two days before? Now those memories felt like bruises deep within her. Her sense of loss was as real as the bone-chilling January wind.

"Take a seat." She was squeaking again. She might as well wear a sign: EMOTIONALLY DISTRESSED.

He sat down on the swing next to her, hooking his arms around the chains. He was quiet for a moment, tipping his head back and staring into a cloudless sky. Nicki did the same, then in unison they turned to look at each other.

"Well?" he asked. "You said you had something important to tell me."

"I do . . . sort of." Nicki hesitated, putting the swing in motion with a nudge of her boot. "You see, I've done something, and I want you to keep an open mind when I tell you about it."

Val frowned, watching the hem of Nicki's black wool coat drag back and forth on the rutted, frozen ground. "What are you talking about?"

"Jimmy Valentine. Well, actually I'm talking about Dylan Lichter. I've come up with a plan that could prove whether or not he's involved in the robberies. But it has to be kept hush-hush if it's going to work. That's why I asked you to meet me here, so we wouldn't be overheard."

Val reached out his hand and stopped her swing, then pulled off her sunglasses. "There," he said. "Now you have eyes. I felt as if I were talking to Little Orphan Annie. What plan are you talking about?"

"It's simple. I let Dylan know today—in the most casual way—that Ambassador Devonshire and his

wife will be out of town this coming weekend. This is
true. I also told him about a very valuable Fabergé
egg Mrs. Devonshire received for Christmas. This is
false, but Dylan doesn't know that. I figured if we
staked out the Devonshires' house, like you did with
the place in Palm Beach—"

"Hold it a minute." Val shook his head as if to clear
it. "You did all this to set Lichter up? I thought you
were on his side."

"I am on his side. I'm just trying to prove once and
for all he's *not* Jimmy Valentine." She looked away,
squinting into a cold steel sky, suddenly close to
tears. "I need to know as much as you do. I don't
have as much confidence in my instincts as I used
to."

Val's eyes darkened with a torment of their own as
they studied her pure profile. "Nicki, the last thing I
want—"

She spoke in a rush: "If he doesn't take the bait,
you can cross Dylan off of your suspect list. Deal?"

Val swallowed hard, looking down at the ground.
His cheeks overheated with a stinging rush of blood.
"This time I involve the police from the beginning,"
he said flatly. "Just in case. I have a friend in the
police department here who's been slipping me information now and then. I'll see if he'll help us out."

"Well . . . that's that." Nicki stood up, brushing
the snow off the back of her coat. She had to keep
talking, or her throat would close up altogether, and
she would expire right there in the playground. "I'll
just wait to hear from you. I guess we should plan on
watching the house the entire weekend. I have a pair
of binoculars. Do you want me to—"

"You're not going to be there."

She glared down at him. "I am."

"Aren't. An insurance investigator will be there, and the police will be there. A gossip columnist just won't be necessary."

"A gossip columnist *will* be there. Either I go with you, or I go by myself, but I will be there. I thought of this whole thing. I deserve to see it through."

Val stood up slowly, a muscle twitching in his jaw. "All right. But you stay in the car, *no matter what happens.* Is that understood? Completely understood, totally and thoroughly understood?"

"Understood."

"One more thing. What if it turns out that Dylan *is* involved? Can you handle that?"

Nicki held his gaze for a long moment before answering. "I've dealt with worse disappointments."

They faced each other in bleak silence, a sun that held no warmth beating on their faces. Then Val slipped Nicki's sunglasses back on her face, touched the tip of her nose with a gentle finger, and walked away.

Nicki's heart was choking her. She sat back down on the swing, head bowed, fingers clenched in her lap. She hadn't meant to say that. What was wrong with her? She felt as if she were two different people, one needing Val Santisi more than ever, one deliberately challenging him.

She thought of herself as a realistic woman. She hadn't expected Prince Charming when she'd finally fallen in love. She'd only wanted a man to trust, to depend on, to feel safe and secure and adored by. A long-awaited answer to those secret, little-girl dreams from long ago on Newton Street.

She stood up stiffly, pulling the collar of her coat high around her face. As she walked to her car, she brooded on the uncertain future. She truly didn't know what to expect from Val Santisi. She knew only that the love was still there, undimmed, stubborn, illogical.

Waiting.

Friday evening an inconspicuous little sedan pulled into a driveway across the street from the Devonshire home. Inside were three dark, puffy shapes, the investigator, the policeman, and the gossip columnist, all wearing goose-down parkas against the cold. You didn't keep the heater running while on a stakeout, the policeman informed Nicki sternly. There was a right way to do these things and a wrong way.

To Nicki's surprise, the policeman turned out to be Sergeant McRoth, the same red-haired fellow Val had mentioned was at the Knight's party.

"He *was* hired for security that night," Val informed her in a grudging voice. "Sometimes I surprise myself and actually tell the truth."

Throughout the long night, Val remained subdued and distant. He seldom met Nicki's gaze. He was very careful and very quiet, a stranger with familiar features. Nicki was relegated to the backseat, given a blanket and a thermos of hot coffee, then more or less forgotten. Val and Sergeant McRoth occasionally conversed in low, hushed voices as they watched the house, binoculars glued to their faces. Despite all the coffee she drank, Nicki fell asleep around 4:00 A.M. Three hours later Val and Sergeant McRoth dropped her off in front of her apartment building.

"Tomorrow night?" she asked, stifling a yawn as she climbed out of the car. Then, when the two men exchanged a grim look, she added sweetly, "Or should I just bring my own car and meet you two there?"

"I'll pick you up at seven," Val muttered.

The next night began as a carbon copy of the first. Same driveway—a friend of Sergeant McRoth's—same seating arrangements, even what tasted like the same coffee. Nicki had brought her own binoculars this time, rather than irritating Sergeant McRoth as she had the night before by asking to borrow his. She kept to herself, her troubled mood growing a bit lighter with every hour that passed. It wasn't Dylan. She'd been right. Everything was nice and quiet, which was just what she wanted.

Until the burglar alarm went off.

The noise seemed to reverberate from all four corners of the Devonshires' property. They must have had alarms installed both inside and outside, judging by the clanging bells that split the night. Nicki could only imagine what it must sound like from inside the house.

Paralyzed with shock, she watched Val and Sergeant McRoth bolt from the car. They each had a gun in hand as they ran across the street, though she had no idea where the weapons had come from.

Don't let it be Dylan. Don't let it be Dylan.

A patrol car arrived almost instantly, siren blaring, adding to the confusion. Another car was right behind. Within minutes, curious neighbors in bathrobes crowded out on their front porches. Nicki's view of the Devonshires' front door was obstructed by a well-trimmed evergreen, but she remained in the car. She wasn't sure she wanted to know what was happening.

Don't let it be Dylan. What have I done?

It seemed like an eternity before she spotted Val's broadshouldered figure walking slowly toward the car. The gun was gone. Even in the dark, she could see the grim set of his expression. Rather than opening the door on the driver's side as she had expected, he opened the back door and stuck his head inside.

"Was it—" she began, but Val cut her off abruptly.

"Did you know the Devonshires had a niece?"

Taken aback, Nicki racked her rattled brain. "Yes, I think they've spoken of a niece. I can't remember her name. . . ."

"Emily?" Val asked flatly.

She nodded, eyes wide.

"And did you know that while the Devonshires are out of town, they asked Emily to house-sit, seeing as how there had been so many robberies lately?"

Gum, Nicki thought. I need gum. "I don't believe they mentioned that, no."

"Emily heard a frightening sound coming from the basement," Val went on tonelessly. "Emily pulled the burglar alarm. Sergeant McRoth and I found a cat trapped in the window well making those frightening sounds. Emily was so grateful, she hugged us both, which was in itself a frightening experience. Emily is not an attractive woman, but she is very strong. The other officers on the scene could hardly contain themselves."

Nicki was very quiet. Then, in a hopeful voice: "We could look on the bright side. At least we know Dylan is innocent."

"He might be. Or he could have been waiting in the wings when Emily scared him off by setting off the alarm. We'll never know, will we? Excuse me. I'm going back to rescue Sergeant McRoth. Emily wants to date him." And with that, Val slammed the door and stalked back across the street.

It was a terrible thing. A nightmare. Nicki's entire plan had backfired. They had learned absolutely nothing. Sergeant McRoth and Val had not only been embarrassed, they had been mauled by an unattractive woman. By all rights, Nicki should be fighting back the tears, overwhelmed with remorse.

She couldn't help herself. She fell back against the seat and started to laugh.

Ten

On Sunday morning, the newspaper ran a humorous little article describing the fiasco at the Devonshires' home. Nicki curled up on the sofa and read the entire thing without cracking a smile. Somehow in the light of day, it didn't seem so funny. Dylan had neither been vindicated nor proven guilty. Val had been thwarted yet again. Poor Sergeant McRoth would never hear the end of it from his fellow officers, and Jimmy Valentine was probably laughing himself sick.

So much for her sleuthing career. If she had any brains at all, she'd do herself a favor and concentrate on ministering to her aching, wounded heart. Maybe it wasn't too late to somehow solve this damnable, falling-in-love mess. Three weeks earlier she'd been a fairly normal woman—discount the bubble-gum addiction—who enjoyed being alone as much as she enjoyed the company of others. She'd been content;

possibly because she hadn't known what she was missing, but content nonetheless. When had life become so complicated, so incredibly frustrating?

So lonely?

Halfway through her second cup of coffee, Philip Rafi arrived at her door, bearing an expensive bouquet of hothouse flowers. He looked breathtakingly debonair in a shapeless gray blazer, pink shirt, and dark gray slacks. Needing comfort as she did, Nicki was wearing her old green robe and her fuzzy bunny slippers. It was a humbling moment.

"Running late this morning?" Philip asked oh-so-politely, his sparkling gaze lingering on the slippers.

"Late? I don't know what . . ." Nicki's eyes stretched, her hands covering her mouth. "The brunch," she mumbled. "You were taking me to brunch at Rino's."

"And I still am," he replied smoothly, handing her the flowers. "Hopefully. I forgive you for forgetting me; I am eminently forgettable. But since I am here and quite hungry . . . ?"

"Just give me ten minutes," she said.

She raced into the kitchen and put the flowers in water, then down the hall to her bedroom. She took a thirty-second shower, her hair tucked up in a plastic cap, then dressed in a knobby beige jumpsuit with a wide leather belt. Her hair was less than sparkling clean; she tugged it back with a huge gold clip and added gold earrings to match. Very little makeup, there wasn't time. She looked . . . passable, but a far cry from Philip's subdued elegance. Love on the rocks, she had discovered, wreaked havoc with one's personal style.

As always, Philip was more than gracious when she walked into the living room fifteen minutes later.

"Breathtaking," he pronounced, kissing her lightly on each cheek. "And I am the luckiest man in Washington to have you at my side today. Shall we go?"

Philip was the perfect companion. He entertained her with pleasant conversation while they dined—no easy feat, since Nicki was lost in thoughts of her own—then spent another hour back at her apartment, drinking coffee in front of a warm fire. It was a civilized, undemanding morning. He was a civilized, undemanding man. When it came time for him to leave, he once again kissed her on the cheek and told her in a concerned voice that she should get more rest. She was looking pale.

Long after Philip had gone, Nicki sat before the fire, staring with unseeing eyes into the flickering flames. If love were something one earned, she thought wistfully, then she would be madly in love with Philip Rafi. He was kind, sincere, a gentleman in every respect. He possessed a wry, subtle sense of humor and a marvelous ability to listen. Worthy of great love, certainly, yet she didn't love him and never had. Which brought her to the conclusion that love was a gift, unearnable, unpredictable, and without conditions. She had given that gift to Val, and he had given it to her. And like any other gift, once freely given, it could not be taken back.

She had once told Val that love wasn't supposed to disappoint you, or leave you feeling alone or frightened. She knew now that wasn't true. He'd hurt her, and she'd hurt him right back, which only proved they were human. Capable of mistakes. Capable of fear.

She wondered what would happen if she went to him right now. If they really talked. Without challenges or ultimatums, just . . . talked. She'd been thinking a great deal about Val's childhood. Like Nicki herself, he'd learned at an early age to look out for his own interests, making the rules as he went along. He was not now and never would be a conventional man. Which, if she were honest, was one of the reasons she had fallen in love with him.

They were both survivors. Nicki followed the rules because it suited her purposes; Val broke them for the same reason. The end results were not so very different. They made their own luck, with their fingers crossed behind their backs. Val loved her— she believed that with all her heart. Now he needed to learn to love himself. It just so happened there was no better person in the world to teach him than Squeaky Boggs.

And fortunately Squeaky Boggs was no quitter.

Heart softly pounding, she stood up and got her coat from the closet. Her destination was the only thing that was clear in her mind. Figuratively speaking, her fingers were still crossed behind her back. Did everyone agonize over the love in their lives? Did everyone doubt and fear both themselves and their lovers before they accepted the inevitable and made a run for daylight?

Probably not. Squeaky Boggs and Val Santisi *never* did things the way everyone else did.

She opened the door to leave and found Val standing in the hallway with his hand raised to knock. It would have been a thrilling moment had he come to her because he couldn't stay away, just as she was going to him, but his expression told a different story. There wasn't a hint of animation in his features. His eyes were darker and more somber than she had ever seen them.

"What is it?" she whispered, still and apprehensive.

He walked in and slammed the door behind him. Hard. "It's bad. Unbelievably bad."

"Tell me."

He took a deep breath and let it out, his broad shoulders slumping beneath the familiar black leather jacket. "You haven't listened to the news tonight, have you?"

"No." Squeak.

"Well, guess what?" He paced over to the window and right back again, his hands pushed deep in the pockets of his coat. "Jimmy Valentine, everyone's favorite burglar, struck again last night. And guess *where* he struck? Believe it or not . . . the residence of *Ambassador and Mrs. Devonshire.*"

Shock rippled over Nicki's features, stole her breath. "What? That isn't possible! When did it happen? What about Emily? What are you talking about?"

"Emily," he said softly. A bitter smile stretched his lips. "I will hate that name forever. Emily. When the Devonshires came home this afternoon, they discovered that Mrs. D. was missing most of the contents of her jewelry box. They called the police, naturally.

One of the boys who responded also happened to have been on the scene the night before. When he asked about Emily, the Devonshires were very confused. You see, they do have a niece named Emily—you were right about that—but she happens to be thirteen years old and living in Omaha."

"Good heavens." Nicki staggered to the sofa and collapsed. "Good heavens. Good heavens."

"More like holy hell," Val said grimly. "We blew it, and we blew it big."

"That means . . . the woman you talked to last night . . . that unattractive woman . . ."

"Let's put it like this. Sergeant McRoth has the thankless distinction of being the only police officer in Washington that Jimmy Valentine has made a pass at."

"Holy hell," Nicki muttered. After that, she was speechless.

Val sat down beside her on the sofa, head bowed, hands dangling between his knees. "Dammit. I lost him—her—again."

Nicki shook her head. "It doesn't make sense. A woman. How would she know the Devonshires were out of town? They kept their trip secret; I didn't tell anyone but Dylan. How would she know?"

"Jimmy Valentine—maybe we should change that to Jenny Valentine—knows everything. I told you, she's a ghost."

"But a *woman* . . . I can't imagine a woman taking all those chances—rapelling off rooftops, breaking into safes—it's so strange. It's unbelievable." Nicki gave a heavy sigh. "What did she look like?"

He laughed bitterly. "She didn't look like a woman

who could dance on rooftops, I'll tell you that. She was overweight and wore this billowing quilted robe that made her look like the mother of Kong. She had frizzy yellow hair that covered half her face, and her cheeks were sort of . . . puffy."

"Mrs. Devonshire wears blond wigs," Nicki said slowly. "Frizzy blond wigs."

"Mrs. Devonshire already identified the wig we found upstairs as hers. Also the robe. You know, I've dealt with a lot of criminals in the past few years, but never one as cool under pressure as this lady. When she mistakenly trips the alarm, she decides to bluff her way out of a tight spot. She puts on a robe, stuffs a pillow underneath, and pulls on one of Mrs. D.'s lovely wigs. A few cotton balls in her cheeks, and she looks like Brando in *The Godfather*. As a finishing touch, Kitty gets tossed into the window well. The whole cover-up probably took all of forty-five seconds. Damn, what an *idiot* I was."

"Don't blame yourself," Nicki said miserably. "Blame me. This whole thing was my idea. I'm the one who spilled the beans about the Devonshires going out of town. This was all my brilliant idea." Then, in a hesitant voice: "I really hate to say this, but . . . is there any chance she was really a he? Any chance it might have been—"

"Dylan?" Val shook his head. "The lady hugged me. Certain parts of her were definitely real. Besides, we checked on Dylan's whereabouts last night. He worked at the paper with a couple of other reporters till midnight, then they all went back to Dylan's place and played poker till dawn."

"They do that every Sunday night," Nicki said. "Dylan's social life is limited to his family, the boys in the newsroom, and his weekly date with Serena Grace. He may talk a lot, but he talks to the same people over and over again. I think Serena Grace is probably the most exciting thing that's ever happened to . . ."

She never finished the sentence. The shock of realization hit them both like high voltage. Val's dark eyes met Nicki's blue ones. Someone gasped.

Serena Grace, Val thought, remembering that well-endowed hug. Some things couldn't be faked.

Serena Grace, Nicki thought, remembering her amazing coordination. If she could work miracles with Hula-Hoops, she could dance on rooftops.

"Damn!" Val roared, jumping to his feet. "What a bloody *idiot* I am!"

Fortunately Nicki had once dropped Dylan off at Serena Grace's apartment. She gave Val directions, and he drove the rental car like a bat out of hell.

Serena Grace's apartment was on the top floor of an old Georgian town house badly in need of a face-lift. The front porch was rotting, the stairs creaked, the wallpaper was curling and smelled of mold. Everything was depressingly run-down . . . until they opened the door to the apartment on the third floor.

It was spotless. It was absolutely beautiful. A Persian rug covered the parquet floor, walls and ceilings were decorated with carved moldings, the furniture was an eclectic combination of antique and contemporary. Elegant wall hangings and artwork bore witness to the exquisite taste of the owner.

Dylan Lichter was sitting on the floor in the middle of the living room, his long legs crossed Indian-style. His shoulders were wilted even more than usual.

"Hey, guys," he said. "I kind of figured you'd be along."

Nicki gave Val a confused glance, then slowly walked over to Dylan. "What are you doing here? Where is Serena Grace?"

"Well, I'll tell you." He took off his glasses, knuckling his eyes. "After Val questioned me this afternoon, I started putting two and two together. Finally. Serena Grace was the only one I told about the Devonshires' trip to Los Angeles. I didn't want to believe she was the one behind all the robberies, but the evidence was pretty hard to ignore. I came straight over, but I was too late. All her clothes are gone. *She's* gone." He put his glasses back on, looking around the room with a curious sort of smile. "I always wondered how she could afford all this. She told me she saved her tips. Besides, I knew she had other friends, wealthy friends. Calvin Fleming, for one. Serena Grace is the kind of woman you liked to give presents to."

"And you didn't mind?" Nicki asked softly. "About her other . . . friends?"

"Why should I? Serena Grace is also the kind of woman who enjoys getting presents. I'm not exactly the wealthiest man in Washington. I just felt lucky she wanted to be with me at all."

"Calvin Fleming," Val muttered, sinking down on the floor beside Dylan. "Of course, that explains it. I couldn't figure out how Jimmy Valentine got all that loot out of Fleming's house the night of his party without my seeing anything."

Dylan nodded. "Yeah. I figured that one out too. Serena Grace made discreet visits to Fleming's home a couple of times each week. The night of the party, no one saw her take anything out of the house because she *didn't* take anything out. She just hid it all somewhere, then took it out with her little by little when she visited. Serena Grace always did carry gigantic purses," he added reflectively.

Nicki sighed and sat down beside them both. For a long while no one spoke. "I don't know what to say to you, Dylan," Nicki murmured finally. "I'm so sorry I ever doubted you. When I told you about the Devonshires leaving town, I just wanted proof that you were innocent. I wouldn't blame you if you never spoke to me again."

"Are you kidding me?" Dylan gave her a rueful smile. "I'm flattered you would even consider me capable of such derring-do. Look at this scholarly face, this adorable but puny body. I might be mistaken for a milkman or a math teacher, but a cat burglar? The mind boggles."

"I suppose I owe you an apology as well," Val said. "I'm the one who first told Nicki not to trust you."

"No problem," Dylan replied kindly. "I told her the same thing about you. I guess Serena Grace had us all going around in circles."

Nicki put her hand on Dylan's arm, wanting to offer some sort of comfort. "You must be devastated.

Dylan, try not to blame yourself. You couldn't know. Serena Grace was using us all for her own purposes. Don't torture yourself with regrets."

Dylan looked surprised. "I'm not tortured," he said, as if he couldn't understand where she had got that idea. "Hell, I just had the best three months of my life."

Eleven

Hell's bells, there was a burglar in his apartment.

Val couldn't believe his lousy luck. Serena Grace had skipped town, and six months of his hard work had skipped town right along with her. He and Dylan had been taken to police headquarters to give their statements, a process that had lasted for nearly three hours. He hadn't seen Nicki since she'd taken a cab home from Serena Grace's apartment.

And now the final, ironic straw. Just when he wanted to crawl into bed and brood over his miseries, this had to happen. The door to his apartment was slightly ajar, the lock obviously having been forced open. And a damn poor job the burglar had done; there were so many gouges around the lock, it looked as if he had gone at it with a jackhammer. There had to be a waiting list of criminals who wanted to make Val Satisi's life a living hell.

He took his gun from his shoulder holster, clicked

off the safety, then took a deep, steadying breath. He really hated this part.

He kicked open the door with a force that sent wood splinters flying. Both arms were outstretched at chest height, the pistol pointed unwaveringly at the burglar in his living room.

The burglar who appeared to be feeding his fish.

The burglar he loved.

Nicki screamed and threw up her hands, tossing the fish food over her shoulder and into the tank, box and all. "Val! It's me! Don't shoot me!"

"I have no intention of shooting you," he snapped, lowering the gun and clicking the safety back on. "But I could have, you little idiot. What are you doing breaking into my apartment?"

"Just a minute." Nicki closed her eyes, panting hard. "I can't breathe. You scared me to death. I need artificial respiration." She opened one eye, squinting at him. "Do insurance investigators know how to do that?"

"No," he said with a growl. "The only thing we know how to do is let our man—or woman—get away. Why are you here?"

Nicki swallowed hard. She had the feeling he wasn't just talking about Serena Grace. "I wanted to see you. You weren't home, so I decided to try my hand at picking your lock. It only took me half an hour. I used my car keys and my nail file and a hair clip."

"A criminal is born." Val took off his jacket and his shoulder holster and put them on the coffee table next to a pile of unmatched socks. Then he looked up at Nicki, his shadowed jaw set. "It's almost one o'clock in the morning. You should be home."

Not an encouraging beginning, Nicki thought. It's a good thing I'm a determined sort.

"Who says?" she asked.

"Who says what?"

"Who says I should be home? I don't want to be home. I want to be here. I didn't expect you would try and shoot me, of course, but I still want to be here."

"I did not try and shoot you." Val closed his eyes, rubbing the rock-hard muscles at the back of his neck. It didn't help. His entire body was thrumming with tension, nerves, and exhaustion. He dropped his voice to a harsh whisper. "Go home, Squeaky. I'm not myself tonight. There are just too many things . . ."

She approached him slowly, staring at the beloved, stark lines of his face. "Too many things . . . ?" she prompted softly.

He opened his eyes, looking at her hair, her lips, the thrust of her breasts beneath her clothes. "Too many things I've lost," he said.

Love and empathy turned her heart over in her chest. She touched his face wonderingly, tears putting a diamond sparkle of light in her deep blue eyes. "I once told you that love wasn't supposed to disappoint you, or leave you feeling alone." Her voice had a husky plea in it, and more than a few squeaks. "I was wrong, Val. We both made mistakes, but that only means we're human. You haven't lost me. I pray to God I haven't lost you."

For a moment she saw it all in his fallen-angel eyes: the love, the relief, the white-hot desire . . . and then it was gone, as if a dark curtain had closed over a lighted window. "You should go home, Squeaky," he said in a dull, passionless voice. "There's nothing for you here."

She watched his withdrawal, biting her lip. "You're wrong. *You're* here."

He felt himself weakening, drying up and crumbling inside. He stepped back and back, until he came up hard against a wall. He needed the support. "I rest my point," he said. "I'm here."

She stared at him for the longest time. Her lips tightened. Her eyes caught fire. Her hands and arms started to tremble. Then, very deliberately, she walked up to him and slapped his cheek . . . *hard*. "Snap out of it, Santisi! Fight for me! I'm the best thing that ever happened to you!"

"But I'm not the best thing that ever happened to you!" he said explosively. He could still feel the stinging imprint of her hand on his cheek. "I'm not bloody good enough for you, and don't blame me if you're too blind to see it!"

"'Good enough' has nothing to do with love. Love doesn't guarantee we won't make mistakes, but it gives us a reason to keep on trying, no matter what happens. *No matter what*." She took a shaky breath, her blue eyes swimming. A single tear rolled down her cheek. "That's what I want from you, Val. A promise that you'll keep on trying. I can't settle for less, I can't . . . it hurts too much."

Val swallowed hard. His vision was softly unfocused, and his voice wouldn't work right. "I don't ever want to hurt you. You deserve the best things . . . the very best things. . . ."

"I deserve the same thing you deserve, the same thing everyone deserves. I deserve acceptance. And the only person in the whole world I want it from is you."

He tipped his head, looking troubled and wary and the slightest, the *slightest*, bit hopeful. "What do you see in me?" he whispered.

"My dearest friend," she said with quiet emphasis. "My love. My family."

"Family . . ." For the first time he allowed himself to touch her, putting his palms on her tear-wet cheeks. His thumbs stroked the wetness away, over and over again. He couldn't quite grasp the fact that he was going to do it, to allow her to believe in him and have faith in him. It was terrifying, but not nearly as terrifying as the alternative.

"I'll try to be good enough," he whispered. "For you, Squeaky . . . I think I could be just about anything."

Nicki threw herself into his arms, bumping her nose hard on his chin and stepping on his foot. It didn't matter. Val Santisi and Squeaky Boggs *never* did things the way everyone else did.

"We're going to be all right." Her voice was soggy and trembling with relief against his shoulder. "We're together. We're going to get what we deserve, you and I."

He pressed a kiss and a shaky smile against her hair. "Heaven help us."

"It will."

Epilogue

Nicki offered to move to New York. She had a reputation of sorts; she could write anywhere. Besides, she thought she might like to try her hand at serious journalism. The rich and egocentric would get along just fine without her.

Val offered to stay in Washington. He said the criminals could get away from him there as well as anywhere, but he said it with a smile. So they compromised, deciding to start fresh in their own unique way. They opened a world atlas to a map of the United States. Nicki covered her eyes and plopped her finger down on the map, fervently hoping they weren't going to end up in the middle of Lake Superior. Fortunately her finger landed smack-dab on the city of Santa Fe, New Mexico. Neither of them had ever been to New Mexico, but it was bound to have newspapers and criminals. It was also bound to have its fair share of justices of the peace.

They spent Valentine's Day packing up everything in Val's apartment. They had just taped up the last box when a messenger arrived, delivering a large, paper-wrapped parcel with Val's name on it.

"More presents?" Val asked Nicki. "You already gave me twelve new wallets so I'd have a place for all my fake I.D.'s."

"That's not from me," Nicki said. "Is there a return address?"

"I don't see one. Clever detective that I am, I think I'll open it up and see who it's from."

He sat down on the sofa to open the box, Nicki looking over his shoulder. Inside the large box was a smaller, heart-shaped box. Nicki was expecting to see chocolates when Val removed the lid. She wasn't expecting to be blinded with a dazzling array of diamonds, emeralds, rubies, and pearls.

"What the . . . !?" Stupefied, Val picked up a necklace, a glorious design of grass-green Colombian emeralds. A necklace he knew only too well. "This is the necklace I was hired to recover in Palm Beach. The necklace Serena Grace stole."

"What? You're absolutely sure?" Nicki was squeaking for all she was worth.

"Positive." Val shook his head helplessly. "The rest of the jewels . . . I don't recognize. What's going on here?"

"What's that underneath?"

"I don't believe this." It was a Mickey Mouse valentine, identical to the ones he'd passed out to his friends in grade school. "Listen, Squeaky. There's a message on the back:

"'The Devonshire jewels—which I am returning to

you—are paste. I was very disappointed . . . they must not be as wealthy as everyone thinks. The emerald necklace, as you know, is the real thing. Take it with my compliments. You came closer than anyone else to catching me . . . twice.

"'Forgive me for leading you on such a merry chase, but you know how it is. A girl has to take care of herself.'"

For a moment neither of them spoke. Val looked over his shoulder at Nicki, and Nicki looked down at Val. He got a crooked grin; so did she. A minute later they were doubled over with laughter.

"What a woman," Val gasped out. "Damn, what a woman. But she can't hold a Hula-Hoop to you, Squeaky, my dear," he said just before he silenced her laughter with a kiss.

THE EDITOR'S CORNER

There are certain stories we all know and love, whether they're fairy tales, classic novels, or unforgettable plays. We treasure them for the way they touch our heart and soul, make us laugh or cry—or both—and next month LOVESWEPT presents you with a bounty of **TREASURED TALES**, six wonderful romances inspired by beloved stories. With special messages from the authors and gorgeous covers featuring black-and-white photographs that reflect the timelessness of these stories, **TREASURED TALES** are worth a king's ransom!

Starting the lineup is Helen Mittermeyer with **'TWAS THE NIGHT**, LOVESWEPT #588, a stirring version of **BEAUTY AND THE BEAST**. It was on Christmas Eve that Rafe Brockman and Cassie Nordstrom first met, but then they parted as enemies. Now, years later, fate brings them together again on Christmas Eve, and they learn that the gift of love is the true Christmas miracle. A heartwarming story from one of the genre's most popular authors.

In **THE PRINCESS AND THE PEA**, LOVESWEPT #589, Fayrene Preston gives her heroine something more intriguing—and gorgeous—to deal with than a troublesome legume. Though Cameron Tate is the perfect hunk to star in a jeans commercial, all Melisande Lanier wants from him is his bed. But Cameron will sell only if workaholic Mel slows down long enough to fall in love with him. Fayrene's winning charm makes this enchanting story shine.

Like Sydney Carton in Charles Dickens's *A Tale of Two Cities,* Nick Atwell is a rebel with a taste for trouble, but his **RENEGADE WAYS,** LOVESWEPT #590 by Terry

Lawrence, can't dissuade Connie Hennessy from believing the handsome diplomat might be just the hero she needs. And she quickly lets Nick know she's willing to barter heated kisses for Nick's help in a perilous mission. Terry really lets the sparks fly between these two characters.

With **NIGHT DREAMS,** LOVESWEPT #591, Sandra Chastain gives us a hero as unforgettable as the Phantom from *The Phantom of the Opera*. No one knows the truth behind the legend of Jonathan Dream, the playboy who'd vanished after building an empire. But when Shannon Summers is taken to his castle to help his disabled daughter, she learns of his scars and his secrets—and burns with the wildfire of his desire. Sandra tells this story with stunning force.

Snow White was contented living with the seven dwarfs, but in **THE FAIREST OF THEM ALL** by Leanne Banks, LOVESWEPT #592, Carly Pendleton would like nothing better than for her seven loving, but overbearing brothers to let her have her own life. Longtime friend Russ Bradford agrees, especially since he has plans to claim her for his own and to taste the sweetness of her ruby-red lips. Leanne delivers a wonderfully entertaining read.

Peggy Webb will light up your day with **DARK FIRE,** LOVESWEPT #593. Although Sid Granger isn't as short on looks as Cyrano de Bergerac, he doesn't dare court the beautiful Rose Anne Jones because he thinks he can never match her perfection. Instead he agrees to woo her for a friend, but the thought of her in another man's arms sends the fighter pilot soaring to her side. Peggy has once again created an irresistible, sensuous romance.

On sale this month are four fabulous FANFARE titles. From *New York Times* bestselling author Amanda Quick comes **RECKLESS,** a tale of a tarnished knight, a daring maiden, and a sweet, searing, storybook love. When

Phoebe Layton needs help to carry out a quest, she can imagine no one more suited to the job than Gabriel Banner. But the Earl of Wylde has a quest of his own in mind: to possess Phoebe, heart and soul.

The Delaneys are here with **THE DELANEY CHRISTMAS CAROL!** For this long-awaited addition to this enduring family's saga, Kay Hooper, Iris Johansen, and Fayrene Preston teamed up once again, and now we're thrilled to give you three tales of three generations of Delaneys in love and of the changing face of Christmas—past, present, and future. Enjoy our special holiday offer to you.

If you missed Tami Hoag's novel **SARAH'S SIN** the first time around, you can pick up a copy now and discover a warm, moving story of two cultures in conflict and two hearts in love. Matt Thorne is every fantasy Sarah Troyer has ever had. And though there's a high price to pay for giving herself to one outside the Amish ways, Sarah dares to allow herself a brief, secret adventure in the arms of a forbidden man.

Maureen Reynolds has been described by *Romantic Times* as "a very HOT writer," and the tempestuous historical romance **SMOKE EYES** will show you why. Katherine Flynn has worked hard to overcome the double prejudice she faced as a woman and an Arapaho half-breed, but she can't win against the power of desire when Zach Fletcher abruptly returns to her life.

Also on sale this month in the Doubleday hardcover edition is **CONFIDENCES** by Penny Hayden. In the tradition of Danielle Steel, **CONFIDENCES** is a deeply moving novel about four "thirty-something" mothers and a long-held secret that could save the life of a seventeen-year-old boy.

Well, folks, it's around that time of year when people usually take stock of what they've accomplished and look forward to what's ahead. And one of the things we've been taking stock of is **THE EDITOR'S CORNER**. It's been a continuing feature in LOVESWEPT books since LOVESWEPT #1 was published. That makes almost ten years' worth of previews, and we wonder if it's still something you look forward to every month, or if there's something else you'd like to see perhaps. Let us know; we'd love to hear your opinions and/or suggestions.

Happy reading!

With warmest wishes,

Nita Taublib
Associate Publisher
LOVESWEPT and FANFARE